BEAUTIFUL EVIDENCE

LEONA WHITE

Copyright © 2025 by Leona White

All rights reserved.

No part of this book may be reproduced in any form or by any electronic or mechanical means, including information storage and retrieval systems, without written permission from the author, except for the use of brief quotations in a book review.

❧ Formatted with Vellum

ALSO BY LEONA WHITE

The Roma Syndicate

Painted in Sin || The Marriage Debt || Beautiful Evidence

Mafia Bosses Series

The Irish Arrangement || The Last Vendetta

The Constella Family

Under His Protection || Under His Watch || Under His Control || Under His Embrace

The Baranov Legacy

LEONA WHITE

Guarded Rebellion || Savage Surrender || Shielded Secrets || Defiant Devotion

Holiday Mafia Standalone's

Velvet Deception || Twin Deception

BLURB

He's here to cage me.

But his eyes say *he wants to devour me.*

Vincenzo Morelli—syndicate enforcer,

and now, my personal shadow... and sin.

They told him not to touch me.

So he did it with his tongue instead.

I'm the daughter of a traitor.

The one secret worth killing for.

He guards me like I'm fragile.

But he breaks me like I'm his favorite weapon.

Each time he says my name,

it sounds like a prayer... or a threat.

I dig up evidence. He buries bodies.

But now we're both choking on the same lie.

The closer I get to the truth,

the deeper I fall for my enemy.

And when I finally uncover what they all fear—

will he save me... or slit my throat while whispering he loves me?

Author's Note: A slow-burn dark, dirty mafia romance where obsession bleeds into desire. If you love tortured heroes, smart heroines, and love that destroys before it heals... Then welcome to ***Beautiful Evidence.***

1

ALESSIA

There isn't an intake sheet, no signature logged—just a body zipped into a black vinyl bag, reeking of disinfectant. It's not the first time an untagged body has shown up and probably won't be the last. I don't hesitate or dwell. Instead, I wash my hands, prepare my instruments, and focus on the task ahead. This is the job—methodical, controlled, and free of sentiment. Every motion is part of the procedure and I signed up for it.

The gurney waits in my suite by the time I push through the morgue doors. Light pulses from the overheads, flickering slightly. My badge shifts against my chest as I walk, a soft tap with every stride. I use it to swipe myself into the secure area.

The air snaps cold against my skin, saturated with bleach and citrus solvent, but beneath the surface, the scents of blood and decay curl through. Death never scrubs clean. It clings.

A morgue tech I don't recognize is peeling off her gloves. She looks up at me and tosses them into the waste bin as I walk closer, then nods toward the gurney. "There's no paperwork, and the body was transferred from Monteverde. He arrived without ID, without personal effects. He's being logged as a John Doe, and they need him processed before noon."

Whoever "they" are, it isn't the police or any hospital. It's the other kind of authority—the kind with teeth, with deep pockets, with the power to make problems disappear before the questions even begin. Men like my father.

I glance at the bag and already feel the nausea coil in my gut. Recognition lands before the zipper opens to reveal a face—Matteo Vescari. A foot soldier for the Bianchi Family—a runner. I saw him once, smoking outside a warehouse while my father negotiated leverage behind closed doors. He looked bored then. Now, he looks like an omen.

"Thanks," I grunt at the tech and force a plastic smile as she ducks out through the swinging double doors and I'm left alone.

I sigh hard and stare down at the half-open bag. I left that life behind a long time ago, and still it finds ways to come back and haunt me. It isn't the first time I've had to autopsy a victim like this, but that doesn't mean I'm comfortable with it.

His face is destroyed, bottom lip split open. Blood is crusted along one ear. His eyelids are swollen and purpled. Ligature marks circle his wrists, the skin beneath broken and red. His forearms are cut with defensive wounds. One finger bends the wrong direction, snapped through the knuckle.

It's not going to be easy to document all of these injuries, and I'm sure I'll find more as I process the body. Men like this ooze secrets as the work unfolds. I wonder what secrets Matteo has to share with me.

The overhead camera blinks red. I glance at it briefly and remind myself that everything I do here is on record. It's meant to protect us—me, the facility, the bodies. There's no privacy in this line of work, and maybe that's for the best.

I tie my hair back, pull on my gloves, and take a long breath to steady myself before I begin. My tools are laid out in perfect rows, each one gleaming under the light—scalpel, forceps, bone saw—all sterilized and ready.

I unzip the bag slowly and lift the edges down around the sides of the gurney. His skin is cold, pale, mottled with early signs of lividity. I check his pockets—empty, as expected. I swab for trace and log any external debris before beginning the external exam by removing his clothing. When I scrape under his fingernails, I collect dried blood—small, dark flakes that fall into the tray in an irregular scatter. It's not his. The DNA will belong to someone else.

After finishing the preliminary notes, I wash the body down. I've done it a hundred times. The water is lukewarm, the cloth smooth against skin that no longer reacts. As I wash him down, the cloth drags over something unexpected. I stop and adjust the light, narrowing my focus.

There, on the surface of his abdomen, is a mark carved into the skin. It's shallow, clean, placed with intention. It doesn't look like the work of frenzy or an accident. The depth is measured—just enough to leave a message without causing fatal blood loss. It's intentional, a symbol I recognize instantly, carved like a calling card.

The carving forms a circle, bisected by a vertical line, with a jagged arc cutting across them both. I freeze in place as my breath tightens, every nerve pulling taut with recognition.

My lungs pull tight. I've seen this before, a memory buried so deep it shouldn't have surfaced, but it does. I was twelve when I saw my father carve that same mark into a man's chest and leave him to rot in the countryside. He thought I was asleep. He never knew I'd watched.

No one has used that symbol in over a decade, at least not to my knowledge. It belonged to a part of the syndicate long thought dead, a piece of the past meant to stay buried.

Why bring it back now?

I document the wound. My hands tremble slightly as I photograph the angles and measure the depth. The cuts weren't rushed. They were slow, meticulous, meant to be understood. This doesn't read like revenge for betrayal. It feels older, more personal—like a reminder sent to settle a score long left open, a warning etched into skin to keep the past alive.

Shaken, I switch to his hands to let myself relax a little. The wrists are torn where restraints were tightened past what is cruel. The bruises arc in neat crescents, left by ropes or zip ties. It doesn't look like the calculated restraint of professionals. These marks feel personal—driven by rage, sharpened by impulse, left by someone who wanted him to suffer before he died.

My voice comes out in a whisper as I connect to this man's humanity and anchor myself in the reality that he was once a living breathing person. "Who were you fighting, Matteo?" I shake my head and realize I can't procrastinate any more. I have to return to the real work, so I dive into his chest cavity.

My scalpel slices through tissue and sinew. I use the bone saw and chest retractor to hold him open, and then I start my internal investigation.

His heart shows signs of rupture, the surrounding bruising consistent with a sharp, concentrated blow. In his stomach, I find remnants of pasta and tomato sauce, broken down just enough to suggest a recent meal. There's alcohol in his system—cheap red wine—but no trace of sedatives or other drugs. Whatever happened to him, he was fully conscious when it occurred.

I stitch the incision closed, though I know it's only for show.

The thread pulls tight. His chest puckers slightly beneath each loop. The overhead light hisses, the hum as thick as static. I sterilize the table and disinfect the work space, working methodically to eliminate every trace of the procedure. I gather his clothes into an evidence bag and seal it, then label the blood sample and place it with the others for refrigeration. I don't generate a report, and I don't enter his name. I have to think carefully about how to handle this first.

I sit with the file open for a long time, the name staring back at me—placeholder text, nothing real yet. I don't input anything and I don't finalize the record. Instead, I close the file without saving and lock the sample drawer myself.

Matteo Vescari won't show up in any system. His name won't trigger a search. Officially, he never passed through my lab—yet.

Before I can leave the suite, the door creaks open behind me. I turn to find Dr. Luca Bernardi in the doorway, his coat still half-buttoned and a fresh espresso in one hand. He doesn't step inside. The dark circles beneath his eyes suggest another sleepless night. He doesn't ask what I'm working on.

"Get that one wrapped up quickly," he says, his tone clipped but casual enough to sound like a suggestion. It isn't. "They want it logged and done. No deep dives and second-guessing. Just process what you have and move on." He's being colder than normal, but maybe he understands who this man is too. I don't question him, but maybe I should.

His gaze flicks to the covered drawer behind me, then back to my face. "And don't ask questions." He's gone before I can respond, and the door swings shut behind him.

I strip off my gloves, toss them into the bin, and make my way out of the exam suite. My legs are stiff from standing too long, and I flex my fingers a few times to get the blood flowing again. The hallway is quiet, the morgue still in that early stretch of silence before the rest of the world wakes up. I pass through the final set of double doors and head for the office that barely feels like mine—just a room with my name on it and a plain desk.

An envelope waits on my chair, out of place in the sterile order of the room. There's no postage, no seal—just my name, scrawled out by hand. I glance around to see if someone nearby is moving or if maybe I can see who left it, but there isn't a soul in this place but me yet. I get a dose of goosebumps as I bend to pick it up. The paper crinkles faintly as I open the flap and slide out a single photograph.

It was taken yesterday.

I'm outside the café on Via Natale del Grande. My coat is crooked at the collar. My hair hangs damp from the rain. Beside me, unmistakable in his hulking frame and crooked posture, is my father. I never even saw him there. I never knew he was there.

I turn the photo over, already certain the back will be blank. It doesn't need to say anything. The photo itself carries the message, sharp as a blade pressed to my neck. The warning is in the image itself, in the fact that it exists at all. The meaning settles like ash in my throat, choking me.

They know...

I carry it to the sink, grab the lighter I use for lighting candles in my office to help me forget the scent of decaying flesh, and light it up. The flame licks at the edge of the photo. The paper curls fast, edges blackening, image disappearing. First my face, then his. Then nothing but ash.

Now trembling, I wash my hands again because the heat of the water might pull me back into my body. The shock runs over my skin and makes me nauseous. Someone has been watching me. Someone powerful and dangerous, and they sent Mateo here for a reason. Something tells me this is going to get messy fast. I shake myself loose but I can't snap out of it.

The pressure in my chest doesn't lift. The weight settles deeper.

I have no idea what's coming next. Only that something is.

And I'll be damned if I'm going to sit back and let it happen.

2

VINCENZO

They call it fallout, like there was ever going to be a clean end to the Vescari mess.

Matteo's body surfaced less than twenty-four hours ago, and already the higher-ups are scrambling to control the narrative. No one wants to admit the possibility that Gordo Costa made a move against the Bianchis, but the silence around his disappearance makes the betrayal feel real. When people vanish without warning, it isn't because they're innocent.

Emilio sits behind his desk at the back of the trattoria, calmly stirring his espresso with a slow hand. He doesn't look at me right away but his terse anger is simmering under the surface. It always impresses me how he can bottle that rage up and mask it with such intentional control. Men like him are dangerous as fuck.

"You know who his daughter is." His words are pointy, pricking my ears. Gordo Costa's daughter doesn't get a choice in the matter. Fortunately for us, she chose a great profession, and she's naive, thinking that changing her last name will hide her from us. Foolish woman...

I nod at him and he continues.

"She's the one who cut Vescari open," Emilio says, voice low. "If there's something in that body worth hiding, she's already seen it."

"Then she's in a position to screw us," I reply. "Even if she doesn't realize what she's looking at." Thinking of how Gordo crossed his brother boils my blood. Emilio is our Don, the man half of Italy reports to. Gordo has now gone silent in the wake of this death, and we either cap the flow of blood and right his wrongs, or the whole fucking city will burn.

Emilio nods once with a stony gaze. "Watch her. Get ahead of this before it turns into another fire we can't put out." He smiles faintly, still not meeting my eyes, and nods at nothing. "You know what to do."

I rise as he gestures his dismissal, the conversation already done in his mind. There's nothing left to clarify. I give a short nod and head for the door, the job already taking shape in my head.

The file comes through encrypted less than an hour later to my email. Dr. Alessia Leone, born Alessia Costa. She changed her name when she turned eighteen. Earned her MD and PhD on government grants and sleepless nights. She has no siblings, one living aunt, no children, and no partner. Her best friend is listed as next of kin on her electronic identity card. Everything about her whispers quiet, deliberate, and controlled—a woman who's built her life around routine in a world that feeds on chaos.

Her apartment is in Trastevere, third floor walk-up, no elevator. She has a one-bedroom, one-bathroom, with a small balcony. Probably the type to lock up at night, not realizing men like me have ways of circumventing traditional security measures. She has no clue what's coming.

I read her file thrice. Then I build her cage.

We park the van half a block from her building, tucked behind a defunct florist's shop. I bring in a two-man rotation team—men I trust to watch without interfering. They aren't briefed on who she is, and I don't offer explanations. They're here to observe, not to speculate, and I keep it that way.

The listening devices go in first—her car is clean. I wire a small mic beneath the steering column and leave the interior untouched. Behind the dumpster near her building, I mount another, disguised to blend with the rusted bolts. Corner of the alley gets one to monitor both angles of her comings and goings.

Alessia is still at work when I let myself into her apartment. The lock takes seconds. I've broken into enough apartments to know the rhythm. Her place is as sterile as her file suggests, with clean countertops, shoes lined neatly by the door, and books stacked in precise thematic order.

I install the cameras quickly. One above the hallway mirror right outside her bedroom, another inside a bookshelf, lens hidden between two medical journals. Under her bedframe, I secure a motion-triggered mic. Her laptop is closed, her phone not here. She took it with her. It means I can't clone it.

I leave no trace.

By the time she returns, I'm back in the van with the feed live. She enters the apartment and flips on a light, then locks the door behind herself, turning both deadbolts. Her movements seem cagey, like she's tense or scared. She doesn't glance at the mirror or check the bookshelf, but something shifts in her posture. The adjustment is slight, but I notice the shake of her hand as she goes for a glass of wine.

She powers off her phone and carries her glass of wine into the bedroom.

She walks into the bedroom and sets the wine down on the nightstand, then unbuttons her shirt. Her blouse slips off her shoulders and down her arms. Beneath it, her skin is smooth and pale, untouched by the sun, all lean muscle and clean lines. There's no visible scarring, no piercings, no distractions—just the quiet shape of a woman who maintains her physique well.

She moves with grace and elegance, her posture upright even as she unhooks her bra and steps out of her slacks. Nothing about her is careless or showy. And yet, the way she pauses in front of the mirror for a split second—bare, backlit by the hallway light—holds something I can't name.

I study the sharp line of her spine, the way she seems to float across the travertine. I've surveilled targets for weeks without blinking, but she moves differently from the men I'm typically watching. And her body is arousing, to say the least.

She goes to bed just before midnight, and I pull up the file on Gordo and scroll through the familiar chaos. His betrayal started months ago. He moved assets without permission, withheld payments, rerouted product through unapproved channels. Everyone thought he was getting sloppy. Maybe he was. But maybe he was planning something bigger.

The problem is, no one knows why he ghosted the family. If he left anything—any evidence, even unintentionally—it could break what's left of our alliances. The Bianchis want someone to blame. The Costas want distance. And I'm the one stuck in the middle, watching her every move, waiting for a misstep.

So far, Alessia hasn't made any mistakes, and I tell myself it's because she's sharp. Because she's her father's daughter. But something about the silence in her apartment gets under my skin. She should've been horrified to see Vescari come across her table. She should've been running for the hills by now. But she sleeps peacefully...

I switch off the feed and close the laptop. The image of her standing by the window lingers longer than I want to admit.

This woman is already under my skin and I've not even introduced myself yet.

3

ALESSIA

The air is thick with the warmth of baked bread and the bitterness of brewed coffee. I lean back in my chair and press the rim of the demitasse to my lips, letting the bitter taste linger before I realize the coffee's gone cold. I set it down on the chipped metal table, watching it rock slightly on the saucer beneath the striped umbrella. Around us, the hum of early afternoon conversation and the clink of cutlery echo across the cobbled patio, where café chairs scrape gently against stone and the sunlight filters through vine-covered trellises.

Chiara's voice cuts through my murky haze. "So now Dr. Mancini thinks he's getting the interim chief job. I mean, please. He's been phoning it in since he got his divorce," she says, rolling her eyes.

I nod, trying to follow along, but my brain's still in the morgue where it got the shock of a lifetime. The faint scent of formalin clings to my jacket like normal. It comes with the job. It's been over twenty-four hours since the autopsy, and I've washed my hands five times, but the image of the symbol carved into Matteo Vescari's stomach keeps flashing behind my eyes.

"Earth to Alessia," Chiara says, waving her hand in front of my face. "Are you even listening to me?"

"Sort of," I say as I drag my gaze back to her. "Sorry. I'm just tired." Lying to my best friend doesn't come easily, but it goes with the territory. She knows nothing of my upbringing or past life. It's better that way, safer for her.

She gives me a look—half concern, half annoyance—and pushes her sunglasses higher on her head. They pin her hair back, giving me a full view of her warm brown eyes that bore into me with curiosity. "You've been tired all day. It's not like you to be this out of it," she says.

I swirl the last drop of coffee in the cup, but the ceramic never leaves the plate beneath. "It's nothing," I reply quietly. What can I even say to her? My dad's a higher-up in the Italian Mafia and I left him behind, but he's come back to haunt me? That'd go over like a lead balloon.

"It's not nothing. You're twitchier than usual. And you didn't even complain about the new tech," she points out. It almost draws a chuckle, because I do complain about that tech a lot.

I smile faintly. "She'll quit by next month. They always do," I say.

Chiara grins. "Seriously, if something's going on, you can tell me," she adds. Her fingers wrap around the tea mug in front of her on its own ceramic plate, but there's no way I could open up even if I wanted to. I'm protecting her from things she knows nothing about, and she doesn't even know it.

Avoiding her scrutiny, I glance toward the street, letting my eyes drift across the crowd without focus—until they land on a man standing half-shielded behind a vendor's cart stacked with oranges. He wears a dark coat and has dark hair. He's not pretending not to look at me. He's watching me directly, as if he's waiting for something.

I shift in my seat and tap my spoon on the saucer a few times impatiently. Chiara raises a brow at me and then furrows her forehead.

"Behind me. Across the street. Don't make it obvious," I say under my breath. Then I shift my gaze toward the front of the cafe where my waiter bustles about filling people's coffee cups. I'd like to wave my arm at him and draw his attention, but I don't want the man to realize we're about to leave. I don't want him to follow me.

She stretches like she's adjusting her back, casting a glance over her shoulder. "I don't see anyone," she says, frowning. Then she brings her arms back in front of her, but instead of folding them on the table like they were, she reaches for her purse.

I look again, but now he's gone, which makes my heart rate tick up a few notches. A man watching me is dangerous. A man who was watching me and who is now invisible is deadly.

Chiara frowns. "What am I supposed to be looking at?" she asks. And this time, as she opens her purse and pulls out her clutch, she turns obviously and stares in that general direction. So much for nonchalance.

"It doesn't matter," I say as I lift my cup again, raising it to wave at the waiter. He sees me and nods.

"Creeper?" she asks, turning back and pulling a few bills from her pocketbook. She drops them on the table and sets the corner of her saucer on them so they don't blow away in the breeze.

"Maybe," I reply, keeping my tone casual, though my neck prickles. "Maybe he was just checking you out." My words are meant to be playful, put her at ease, but my voice cracks, belying my anxious tension.

"You're jumpy," she observes, and her shoulders bob. "You sure everything's okay?"

I shrug. "I'm just tired," I repeat, but I know I'm not really selling it. The truth is I am tired. Exhausted, actually. I've spent the better part of my adult life hiding from the men my father calls his family. I broke ties with anything that resembles blood relation when I

BEAUTIFUL EVIDENCE

figured out who they are. What they do… and how deep their reach still goes.

The thought makes my skin crawl, but I try to shake it off.

Then I scan the sidewalk two more times before I stand up to leave, tucking my clutch under my arm.

Chiara pulls out her phone and checks the time. "I've got rounds in twenty. Walk with me?" she asks.

"Sure," I say.

I leave a few coins under my cup, knowing her bills will cover both of our lunches, and head up the block beside her. I keep my chin high, but I'm scanning every surface we pass—windowpanes, polished car doors, anything that might reflect movement. The man's gone, erased like chalk in the rain, but the sense of being watched still coils in my gut. The dread still crawls heavily up my back, whispering that what I saw wasn't a trick of the light.

"Hey," Chiara says, nudging me gently with her elbow. "Are we still on for Via del Corso this weekend? I need new shoes, and I'm not buying anything unless you approve."

I smile faintly, grateful for the normalcy. "Of course. Saturday afternoon?"

She nods. "Text me. We'll grab gelato, but only after you find me the perfect dress for the fundraiser."

At the next corner, Chiara peels off toward the hospital. "Call me if you want to vent about weird men lurking in fruit stands," she says over her shoulder with a laugh, and suddenly, I breathe lighter, like maybe I was just hallucinating. The formalin maybe got to me.

I smile. "Thanks," I reply.

Against my better judgment, I head back toward the café, unsure why I feel the need. Maybe I want to check again. Maybe I want to prove to myself that I didn't make it up. The sidewalk's crowded now with delivery vans, tourists, and a group of nuns laughing with plastic gelato cups in hand. Everything feels normal, loud, and safe.

He's there. Not across the street this time, shadowed by carts or tucked into a crowd. He stands in plain view, two steps from the table I left behind. His posture is too relaxed, like he's waiting for an old friend. And his hands are buried in his coat pockets, which scares me. He could have a weapon.

His gaze locks onto the café door as if he's been rooted to the spot, waiting. When he catches sight of me, he smiles—a quiet, unreadable curve of the mouth that carries a chill. It's not friendly. It's not curious. It's the smile of someone sinister who has been made and doesn't care.

My feet slow without permission, my breath thinning as I take him in, instinct screaming beneath my skin, though I find myself holding my breath instead of calling for help.

He doesn't move until I'm within reach. Then he steps forward just slightly. He's not close enough to touch, but he's close enough that I register his presence.

"Alessia, right?" he says, his tone smooth and confident. He's tall, lean, and unsettlingly composed, with short black hair that doesn't move in the breeze and inky black eyes that crawl with intimidation. A thin line of stubble shadows his jaw, but it's the tattoos that catch my eye— just visible beneath his coat sleeves and in the dip in his neck just where his collarbones meet.

He looks like the type of man who knows where every monster lives, who's done terrible things with clean hands.

My heart jerks. "Do I know you?" I ask, my voice guarded.

"Vinny," he replies and offers a hand, but he doesn't look surprised that I don't take it. "Your name came up in conversation. I figured I'd introduce myself."

"What conversation?" I ask, keeping my eyes on his. All around us, the café pulses with life—glasses clink, silverware scrapes, a couple at the next table dissolves into laughter—but I don't let myself break focus.

"Friends in common," he says with a shrug, like this is a casual run-in and not a carefully calculated approach. "I work in private security. Mostly risk assessments and internal investigations."

I say nothing and let the silence stretch. The noise around us feels far away, like it's happening behind glass or with a mute in place. People are moving, but my eyes stay locked on the snake in front of me coiled to strike.

He gestures toward the table. "May I?" he asks.

"No," I tell him tartly. I'm ready to walk away now and pray he doesn't follow.

He smiles again, but it doesn't reach his eyes. "Fair," he says.

I study him. He looks to be in his early thirties with a lean build and a tailored coat. I see no visible weapon, but his stance suggests training. His eyes are sharp for someone who just happens to work in security.

"What do you want?" I ask.

"To meet you. Make sure you're okay," he says.

"I'm fine," I reply, keeping my expression unreadable. Make sure I'm okay? Is that some fucked up way of saying my father is checking on me? Because that's what this is, right? My father sent me that stiff, and now he's sending his soldiers to follow up and make sure I'm obeying. It's sickening. I move to walk past him, but he gently takes my wrist and I snap my hand away.

"Some people aren't happy about your involvement in recent cases. I thought I'd check in," he says calmly, but there is something eerily terrifying about the way he looks at me, like I'm the next victim.

I tense. "You're not with the police," I say, "so stay the fuck away from me."

"No," he replies simply, "I'm not *polizia*."

"Then why would you care?" I ask. Now my chest is heaving with adrenaline, preparing me to fight. I don't have my mace, no weapon to fight him off. Even if I did, he's twice my size and trained to kill and I am just a fucking medical examiner.

He leans back slightly. "Because a friend cares," he growls so quietly, I'm sure it's the devil himself projecting the words into my brain.

I stare at him. "You're very pushy for a man who wants to reassure me," I say.

He laughs quietly. "You're smart. You don't need the details spelled out, do you?"

I say nothing in response, but I let my eyes turn away from him and stare at the back of the bus where the nuns are boarding with cups of espresso and smiles now.

He pats the back of my shoulder then says, "Take care of yourself, Alessia. Things are moving fast."

Then he's gone, walking away, sliding his hands into his pockets with ease again.

I wait a full minute before I exhale. Then I turn and walk the long way back to the lab, checking over my shoulder every few minutes.

By the time I get back, I'm trembling. The fluorescent lights feel harsher than usual, and every metallic clink echoes through my body, making me jerk. I finish my remaining reports in a daze, barely registering the paperwork or the murmured conversations of passing staff. My coat's on and I'm out the door before anyone can stop me, heart still racing from something I can't rationalize away. That was not a hallucination. That was a message I heard loud and clear.

When I reach my building, dusk is pressing down over Rome. I pause before unlocking the door. Everything looks normal. The same old potted rosemary is still dying on the windowsill. The mail slot's half-jammed with flyers and bills. Nothing appears out of place at first glance.

But the moment I step inside, I know something's wrong. The air feels disturbed. It doesn't feel like someone broke in, but it feels like someone passed through recently.

My apartment is clean because that's how I keep it, maybe unconsciously so I'll know if something looks out of place. Years of terror taught me that. But I check the bedroom and closet. Nothing's missing. Nothing appears to be stolen. I crouch and look underneath the bed. The dust patterns are disturbed and have clearly shifted. Someone has reached under at some point.

I don't call the police because there's nothing they can do—not when nothing's missing, nothing's broken, and nothing technically happened. There's no evidence, no forced entry, not even a hair out of place.

But I know what I felt the second I walked in. I know what it means when the air tastes wrong, when objects sit too perfectly, when silence rings louder than it should. Whoever he is, he was here. And every breath I take now is colder because of it.

"Vinny" was a message, cold and direct, and I don't know what it's supposed to mean. But I know it's not good.

I lock every bolt on the door and pull the curtains tightly shut. Then I sit on the edge of the bed and finally let my hands begin to shake.

4

VINCENZO

Alessia doesn't see me, but I see everything. From where I stand across the street, half-shielded by a storefront awning and the dying light of early evening, I track her reflection in the pharmacy's glass. She's standing at the counter, listening as the cashier explains something about availability. Her fingers tap a quiet rhythm against the strap of her bag.

She buys something small and tucks it away in her purse before stepping back out onto the sidewalk. Her path doesn't take her toward the busier roads near the hospital. Instead, she veers down a narrow lane, one of those local shortcuts people who live here use without thinking. The street isn't lit, not populated, and quiet enough that if she screams, no one will hear.

That suits me just fine.

I follow at a distance. My pace mirrors hers—neither hurried nor lazy. The soles of my shoes make no sound against the uneven stones, and the few people who pass me don't look at me twice. This part of the job is mechanical. Tailing a mark is old hat to me. And this one I don't even have to hide from because she's not running scared or calling the authorities. Smart to a point, but dangerous.

She moves comfortably, though she does glance over her shoulder every so often. It's almost so precise, I can calculate it and duck behind something every time. The way her chin dips and her eyes slide sideways tells me she's not sure what she feels, only that it's uncomfortable. Her instincts are good, but they're not good enough.

She reaches the bend where the alley narrows between two shuttered shops. I move quickly, slipping through a side path and circling around the block, cutting her off as she turns the corner. When she steps into the dim gap between buildings, I'm already there, standing still and waiting.

She startles hard, her bag swinging slightly as her hand dives into it. She sucks in a sharp breath, the sound cutting through the stillness between us like a blade, her body frozen mid-motion as if bracing for impact.

"Alessia," I say, keeping my voice low and even as I lift both hands in the universal signal to stop.

She narrows her eyes and tightens her grip on her bag. "What the hell are you doing?" she clips in shock. I can see her pulse thundering in her neck, eyes wide with fright.

"I'm not here to hurt you," I reply, holding steady.

"You're following me," she counters, and her stance hardens as she braces herself.

"I'm watching you. There's a difference," I say, lowering my hands slowly. I don't want to spook her and make her run because I don't feel like sweating right now.

Her eyes narrow further. "You think that's supposed to make me feel better?" She pulls the strap of her bag up higher on her shoulder and glares at me with eyes of fire.

"I need you to not dig around," I say, my voice firm, measured.

She shifts her weight, planting her feet. I've seen grown men not able to defend themselves in a fight, and here is this dainty Italian beauty standing like she's going to square off with me. Someone taught her well. "Digging around what?" she demands, defiant.

"Matteo Vescari," I tell her, watching for her reaction. She pauses, her fingers tightening on the leather strap. Her eyes are pensive and tight, studying me. She knows why she has to stop digging, which means there's something about Vescari's body that scared her and tipped her off.

"Who sent you?" she bites, and her eyes flick around nervously.

"Does it matter?" Keeping my expression unreadable, I let my shoulders relax and watch her expression change.

"It does to me," she snaps, jaw clenched. She's got brass. I like that. Costa never told me how feisty his offspring is.

I step closer slowly, and she doesn't back away, but every muscle in her body tenses like she might. "You're in over your head," I tell her. "These things don't get resolved in labs or on report forms. You know that, Bella."

"If you think you can intimidate me—" she begins, voice rising.

"I don't," I cut in because I'm not here to intimidate. Emilio sent me to observe and persuade. She can't stamp the Costa name on anything that will point back to us, and she can't stir shit up with the Bianchis, either.

The wind picks up slightly, lifting her hair across her cheek. Without thinking—or maybe with intent—I reach out and brush the strand aside with my pinky. My knuckles graze her jaw as I tuck the hair behind her ear, and she audibly growls.

Her eyes lock on mine with rage and for a moment, neither of us moves. Then her hand snaps up and connects with my face, open-palmed and fast. The sound is sharp in the empty alley and my reaction is faster. I reach for her, almost wrapping my hand around her neck, and then stop myself and pull back.

"Touch me again and I will report you," she hisses as she pushes past me, her shoulder slamming into mine.

I snort and chuckle as I rub my jaw and smirk at her. "Understood," I say, turning to watch her ass sway as she walks up the alley away from me without another word. This job might not be boring, after all.

* * *

It's past midnight when I make it back to the compound. The villa looks quiet, but that never means it's empty. Men on night rotation nod as I pass. The office lights are still on. Emilio doesn't keep banker's hours when blood might be spilled.

I knock once before pushing the door open.

He sits behind the desk, sleeves rolled to the elbows, shirt unbuttoned just enough to show the chain around his neck. A half-empty tumbler of amaro rests near his hand.

"Well?" he asks, raising an eyebrow as he leans forward. Then he turns back to his counting, stacks of cash from the latest fence—some slab of artwork his son took care of.

"She's cautious," I say, stepping inside. I walk across the hand-woven rug to stand by his desk and slide my hands into my pockets. "Solitary... She's not communicating with anyone we know. She goes home alone, spends hours at work. She made a pharmacy stop today, but nothing unusual."

Emilio leans back slightly and lets his hand drum on the desk. "And Gordo?" he asks, eyes narrowing. If Emilio's brother shows his fucking face around here, it will be the last time. The bastard has shaken the wrong tree.

"No sign," I say, shaking my head.

"Still..." Emilio picks up his glass and downs his drink, then slams it down.

"Still," I confirm, but it's a bitter word to spit out. Gordo stirred the pot that was simmering and now the city is a cesspit of boiling sin.

He exhales through his nose with a sharp breath and says, "Did you make contact?"

I nod once and meet his stare without flinching. "Briefly," I answer, "and I warned her not to dig. I'm not sure she's going to listen, though." Alessia Costa might've changed her name and gotten a new profession, but she's not stupid. She knows how we work, and if she knows what's good for her, she will obey.

"She spook easily?" he presses, tilting his glass and eyeing the last dribble in the bottom.

"She's not naive, if that's what you mean," I reply. "She knew someone was following her. She just didn't know who." I lean on the leather armchair across from his desk and look up at the portrait of his father hung above the mantel across the room. Now that was a man who knew how to lead a family. Emilio had big shoes to fill, and his son will carry on that legacy.

Emilio picks up his glass, swirls it once, then downs the few drops left. "You let her walk away." There is warning in the cadence of his voice, but I know it's just the way he is. I'm not letting this one slip away from me.

"It wasn't the time," I say, holding his gaze. "If I clip her wings right now the whole city will erupt. Bianchi wants justice for Vescari and the polizia will be watching. A dead criminal with gang-related suspicion doesn't just show up at a morgue undetected. They're watching. I made a choice."

"It won't always be your choice, Vincenzo. If she makes noise—"

"I'll handle it," I interrupt with a clipped tone, carefully weighing what I say. He's not an easy man to work for but he doesn't want yes men. He wants intelligent soldiers trained to think for themselves and make decisions on the fly.

He watches me a moment longer, then nods. "Until then, stay close. Keep her calm. We don't need her running. We need her quiet." His final word is laced with cloaked meaning.

"Understood, sir." I leave the room without waiting to be dismissed. Outside, the evening has taken on a chill. Somewhere across the courtyard, someone is laughing too loudly. But my mind isn't here.

It's back in that alley, where everything shifted.

It's fixed on the way she looked at me—like I was a stranger she almost recognized, like she already knew I'd come back.

And I can't wait to go back.

5

ALESSIA

The lab carries the sharp bite of ethanol and the weight of old memories I'd rather not have to think about anymore. A chemical sharpness clings to the air that is familiar and oddly comforting. I've spent enough nights here to know which microscope flickers when powered on and which drawer sticks from disuse. This place is mine in ways no other space has ever been. It's clean, methodical, and obedient, completely unlike everything else in my life.

And maybe that's why I like it, because it's the only place that up until the last week has been mine, with no trace of my father's black fingers reaching out to touch me.

I seal the cooler and carry it through the side door of the lab, nodding to the lone janitor buffing the hallway tiles. He doesn't look up, which is good. I don't want questions about where I'm going or what I'm doing. Knowing my father is behind this is bad enough.

The private forensics lab at the university—where I used to assist during my residency—is dimly lit when I enter. My access still works —a miracle or an oversight, I'm not sure which. I place the tubes into the centrifuge and set the timer. Soon, it begins to hum as it spins the blood samples I pulled from Matteo's femoral artery. I've already typed his DNA against Interpol and national databases. There were no surprises there, but the partial profile I couldn't classify is what brought me here tonight.

I settle in, snapping on my gloves. The machine beeps its readiness. I breathe in the stillness and let it steady me. Then I start running the test again, this time feeding in mitochondrial sequences and cross-checking them against legacy records that the government databases won't touch. Results start to populate on the screen. If my strange mystery stalker is any indication, the Mob is into something they don't want made public, and doing anything on a government database will draw them to me like flies to shit.

The university feels safer, or at least that's what I let myself believe—right up until I hear a voice that makes my skin crawl.

"Still hiding bodies in your spare time, Leone?" Luca's voice scalpels through the silence, startling me. I never heard his footsteps approaching.

I don't need to turn to place it. "Dr. Bernardi," I say, not missing a beat as I adjust the monitor and let my hand on the mouse move smoothly as if he didn't just make me pee a little. "I assumed you'd be out charming tenure committees." My former teacher turned state medical examiner is my current boss, who apparently still has ties back to this lab too.

Luca steps into the fluorescent light, smirking as he crosses his arms. The wicked light draws dark shadows on his face, making him look morbid. "They charm easily. You, on the other hand..." he says casually. He looks up at the screen and then down at the cooler skeptically.

"I'm not here to be charmed," I reply, flicking off a switch without looking at him. He already knows what I'm doing. I'm sure of it. But he doesn't know whose blood I'm using or why.

He walks a slow arc around me. "No. You're here after hours, rerunning forensic markers on a corpse already cleared for cremation." I shudder at the idea that he's placing accusations without proof, but if he wanted the proof he could order me to cough it up. "That makes me wonder—what are you really looking for?" His voice lowers as he slouches heavily on the opposite counter, inspecting me for lies.

"Old coursework," I say tightly, locking my gaze on the screen. "Thought I might reference some of the mitochondrial cases for the lecture I'm prepping."

He laughs softly, shaking his head. "That's what they call it now?" he says, lips curling. "Coursework…"

I don't respond, but I keep my face neutral as I gather the printouts and pull up a blank screen, pretending to cross-reference files while willing my heartbeat to slow.

He waits, watching me like a hawk circling a cornered rabbit. "You're not even trying to cover your tracks," he says, voice low and edged with contempt. "You think just because you used your old access card that no one would notice?"

I gather another paper from the printer and keep my tone level. "What do I have to cover up? Besides, if I wanted to cover something, do you think I'd be doing it here?" I flick a gaze up at his sardonic grin and steady my breathing. He won't rattle me if I keep myself grounded. He has no proof of anything, and besides, it's not like he knows who I really am.

He scoffs. "You always did think you were smarter than everyone else. But this is sloppy, even for you." The way he casually crosses his arms and narrows his eyes feels more interrogatory than friendly, but I turn back to my work and try not to get bothered by him.

"I'm prepping for a lecture," I tell him again, but I feel my ears burning hotter than Venus. My heart is thudding so loudly I can feel it in my teeth, but I keep my expression smooth.

He leans forward, resting one hand on the desk, invading my space with his presence. "You're lying to me, Alessia, and I'm going to find out what it is you're hiding."

"Maybe I'm just tired," I say, returning my eyes to the blank screen and clicking through meaningless files. "We can't all be fueled by spite and suspicion, Dr. Bernardi." If he can't see the blood pulsing through the veins in my forehead, I'd be surprised.

He lets out a mirthless laugh, shaking his head. "Just remember—if you get caught doing something illegal, I'm not covering for you." His voice starts to fade as he walks away, and I pinch the bridge of my nose as his back is turned.

"Noted," I say quietly, eyes still on the screen, breath held until he's finally far enough away that I can turn the monitor back on.

He wanders out the door to the other workstation, still feigning disinterest, but I can feel his gaze burning into the back of my neck.

The profile completes, and my pulse stalls. There's a ninety-three percent match to my familial DNA strand. It's one not associated with Matteo and not listed in any criminal registry. But I know this marker. I've seen it before—buried in my own bloodwork, years ago, back when I was naïve enough to think a person could scrub their past clean.

It's Gordo's.

My hands curl around the edge of the table as my eyes pore over more of the results. There is no mistaking at all what this means and it's the proof my mind didn't want to see. I'm so glad I ran this test here and not at work because at least here, there is no link to the samples that can be traced back to me.

My father was there at the scene. Or someone who shares his mitochondrial DNA was—Uncle Emilio, maybe? But he doesn't tend to get his hands dirty anymore, ever since he was named Don.

I strip off the gloves and shut the machine down with a series of practiced keystrokes, my mind already three steps ahead. This changes everything, and it explains too much. The man following me around, the strange image sent to me with my father in the same place at the same time as me even though I didn't see him. And most of all, it explains why I felt like someone was in my penthouse apartment.

After I clean up the Mass-Spec and destroy the samples, I exit the lab and head out the side door into the cool evening air, cradling the results folder beneath one arm. My bag is heavy against my shoulder as I cut across the campus courtyard and out onto the main road. The farther I get from the university, the faster I walk, which gets my pulse high with activity, but the anxiety doesn't help, either.

I glance over my shoulder just once as I reach the edge of campus—and that's when I see the same man from the café. He called himself Vinny. He's several paces behind, head angled slightly like he's just out for a walk, but he's not fooling me. He's following me. I realize it only now, with a jolt of delayed dread, and suspect he's been trailing me since I left the building. Maybe since I left work to come here.

I keep moving faster now, cutting across the street, then down a narrower sidewalk lined with trees and old stone walls. He matches my pace from a distance, never closing the gap but never falling behind, either. It terrifies me because he's not even trying to be covert about it. His boldness is all the more reason to be afraid of him.

I cross at a light, duck down an alley, and pause in front of a pharmacy window to check my reflection in the glass. He's still trailing me, just far enough back to make plausible deniability his shield. But I'm done pretending I don't notice.

I stop walking, turning on my heel to face him before he has the chance to pretend this was all coincidence. The streetlight catches in his eyes as he slows, as if considering whether to pretend he wasn't following me or to admit it outright. He hesitates, just for a breath, then shifts his weight forward and crosses the remaining distance between us.

"Alessia…" My name on his lips is both bone-chilling and alluring. HIs Venetian accent is softer than my Roman one, and the way it curls over his tongue softens me around the edges even when I want to be hard and cold.

Still, knowing who he is makes something inside me bristle. "Are you following me?" I ask, narrowing my eyes.

"Yes," he says simply, holding my gaze. "I told you. There are matters that concern you and I'm here… to watch."

"You were in my apartment, weren't you?" I ask, folding my arms across my chest, my voice calm even though my skin prickles. "You went through my things. That's why you're not bothering to hide now."

"Would you believe me if I told you the truth?" he replies, a faint smirk touching his mouth. The light is fading fast, but even in the dusky calm settling over Rome I notice the strong line of his jaw, the curiosity in his eyes.

"Try me," I say coolly, refusing to back down. I cross my arms over my chest, partly to hide the fact that I'm feeling a little flustered. He's good-looking, but he's scary. I know my father would never send someone to watch me who would actually harm me, but letting myself fall for his charm will only come back to bite me later.

He moves closer with unhurried steps. "Your father sent me. He wants eyes on you," he says, and I notice a glint in his eyes, no doubt some sort of perverted thought he's having about me. Men like him are all the same.

My jaw tightens. "Of course he did," I mutter, lifting my chin. I didn't need Vinny's confession to know what my father is up to. I'm going to be forced to bury the truth and jeopardize my career. I knew I should've moved to Paris.

"You're not safe." The tone he uses is edged with warning, though I don't believe he actually cares one fucking lick about me or my safety. He's hired to do a job, and so long as his job is done, he will be paid.

"From whom?" I scoff, matching his steps by moving forward. He thinks he can corner me and make me feel intimidated by him, but I'm not going to cower.

He doesn't answer. Instead, he studies me with those dark, unreadable eyes like he's cataloguing the slope of my spine and the tilt of my head. His tongue draws over his lower lip. His eyes blink slowly. Then he says, "You need to stop digging, Alessia."

"Is that a threat?" I snip before I scoff again and snort out a laugh. "Because I'm sure by now, you know who my father really is and what he's capable of doing." I stare directly into his eyes and his words slice down my spine in a cold chill.

"No. It's a warning."

"I don't respond well to warnings," I say coldly. Though inside, my stomach is roiling now. If he's warning me, maybe he isn't working with my father. I can't name all the criminal families in Rome, but I know the Costas aren't the only ones.

He steps closer, and his fingers lift and graze the side of my jaw like he's moving a hair or smoothing my tears away. It's a soft, gentle touch that warms me down to my chest, then creeps into my belly and settles it. The goosebumps I should feel fly to my stomach to join the butterflies dancing, and before I think, I act.

"Don't touch me," I snap, slapping his hand away.

Vinny chuckles and winks at me before saying, "Ciao, Bella. Try not to dream of me tonight."

I push past him, spine straight and chin high. My steps echo off the courtyard stones. I don't look back, but I'm not foolish enough to believe he's left me alone. Whoever sent him to intimidate me would be very disappointed if he did, and so I know every time I leave my apartment from now on, he'll be there. At least until the public prosecutor has their suspect and the case moves on from my docket.

Later, I lock the door to my apartment behind me and double-check every window, even though I know he's long gone—or at least pretending to be. The lights stay off as I step into the kitchen, unspooling my scarf and tossing my bag onto the counter. I don't bother eating. I'm too keyed up. My fingers twitch like they're still bracing for another shock. I've had a few today already.

I head to the bathroom and splash water on my face. My hands tremble with nerves and my mind replays the conversation with Luca and then the one with Vinny—whose name I'm sure is Vincenzo or something stupid. I think of all the things I should have said to both of them but couldn't conjure up in the moment.

When I finally peel off my clothes and sink into bed, the sheets are cool against my skin, but my jaw still tingles where he touched me. I press the side of my face into the pillow, willing it to erase the memory, but it doesn't help.

His touch lingers like heat after a flame, seared into nerve endings I can't shut off.

I bury my face in the blanket and squeeze my eyes shut.

And I hate that I want to feel it again.

6

VINCENZO

The safehouse sits on the edge of the city, tucked between a row of empty buildings with nothing to mark it from the outside. Inside, everything is sterile—metal, screens, and silence. I've spent too many nights like this, lit only by the glow of a dozen monitors. Rome is a lot like New York City—never truly going to sleep, but Alessia does. It's where she is now, curled in her bed with her creamy skin covered in a white satin sheet, her light snoring coming across the airwaves.

Her apartment flickers across the main monitor. The monitor shows high-definition footage streaming in real time, captured through the network of bugs I installed throughout her apartment last week, long after Gordo's original wiring was removed when she remodeled. She hasn't found my handiwork, or maybe she did and gave up trying to fight it, like the rest of Gordo Costa's legacy.

She hasn't moved in nearly ten minutes—no tossing or restlessness, no sudden shifts. Just the steady rise and fall of her chest as she breathes. Her hair spills across the pillow like ink, tangled from being unbrushed, and I itch to run my fingers through it. Even in sleep, she's beautiful. I study her face and see how much she looks like Gordo and even Emilio. How she thinks she can evade being recognized is beyond me.

She hasn't told anyone about what she knows. Not a single detail has slipped past her lips. She hasn't said a word about the strange symbol carved into Matteo's chest, a detail that should have raised questions immediately—one I only know because it's Gordo's trademark. She also hasn't breathed a word about the bloodwork she ran—not the official results and definitely not the second set I saw her process in secret in that old university lab. She's calculating and deliberate—smart in ways that make people like her unpredictable and hard to manage. That's what makes her dangerous—she got her wit from her father.

I switch feeds on the surveillance system, letting the screen shift with a soft flicker of static. I switch to camera three, which is aimed directly at her laptop screen, zoomed close enough to catch the details. It's encrypted with decent protection, but I've broken into tighter systems for far less compelling reasons.

She's logged into a private research drive. It's not the kind of drive the university IT department monitors or archives. It exists off the books, private and hidden for a reason. It's something older, probably predating her employment, and it feels personal—designed to keep certain work separate from official records. Maybe it's hers, a homemade NAS or something, but definitely crackable.

I lean forward, fingers skimming keys as I slice through the firewall. It takes less than two minutes to break in and mirror the data. The files reveal mitochondrial chain analyses, detailed cross-referenced alleles, and a partial male DNA profile connected to a third, unidentified genetic strand. It makes me wonder who it is and why she went to such great lengths to hide it.

It belongs to someone unknown, a ghost in the system with no official trail. The DNA doesn't belong to Matteo, which means she found it on him—probably defensive—and it can't be found in any official government registry or database.

"Fuck," I mutter under my breath. I rub the heel of my palm against my jaw, staring hard at the screen as if sheer will might change what I'm seeing. If she matches that to Gordo, we're sunk.

This confirms what Emilio was afraid of. There was a third man in the room when Matteo died—one the government hasn't identified. One who could tie the scene to our larger network. If that profile leaks to the wrong hands, the task force doesn't just have a corpse. They have leverage.

Gordo got sloppy. He let he fucker touch him, and not just touch him, but draw blood.

I tap the mic. "We have a problem," I say, knowing Emilio won't appreciate the understatement. I lean back in the chair and crack my neck. The tension settles in like a weight across my shoulders.

"Go on," he growls through the static. His voice buzzes through the earpiece like gravel, and I hear the edge to his voice.

"She found a second profile—unmatched DNA. If Greco gets her hands on that, it opens the 416-bis case." I click through the mirrored files again, double-checking the markers just to be sure I haven't misread the data.

There's a beat of silence before Emilio speaks again. "Bernardi?" he snaps. The name alone sounds like a loaded weapon coming from his mouth.

"She hasn't told him. But he's sniffing around." I glance toward the surveillance footage, watching her turn over in bed. Her leg stretches out across the top of the covers, revealing the curve of her bare hip. My eyes are glued in an instant.

"Shut him up." The words come flat, automatic, like he's ordering a drink, not a body.

I hesitate before I answer, because this is a touchy time. It's not a question of willingness—I'll do it if needed—but the timing has to be precise or it'll backfire.

"If he goes quiet now, it'll raise more flags than it kills. Let me handle it." I rest my fingertips on the desk, keeping my voice level even though I already know Emilio hates delays. My eyes drift over Alessia's form and I imagine what she looks like beneath that sheet.

He leaves another pause, like he's thinking about what I'm saying, then he says, "You have one day." His voice cuts off clean, and silence follows. The line goes dead, leaving behind a myriad of things for me to think about.

I know how important it is to put a lid on the pot so the authorities don't tie Gordo back to the victim because if they do, the Bianchis won't stop until they've destroyed every single one of Emilio's men, including me. But I can't just take out the man responsible for helping head the investigation. It's dumb at best, deadly at worst.

My eyes stay on her body, memorizing every shift under the sheets. But I tear myself away and scroll back through the mirrored files again, scanning the DNA strands and mitochondrial markers with mechanical focus, as if repetition might settle the unease in my chest.

Once I've confirmed the data again, I switch feeds. This time, I queue up the earlier footage from the night—the clip where she came home and changed. I watch as she unbuttons her blouse and peels it off, folding it with unconscious precision before reaching for the hem of her skirt. The camera catches everything—how methodical she is, how unaware. Or maybe she isn't. Maybe she knows I'm there, and this is her way of holding power without saying a word.

I rewind the clip to the beginning and watch the entire sequence play out again—her movements smooth, her posture unhurried, her hands steady. I scrub through the feed frame by frame, pausing on the moment she steps out of her skirt, the moment she bends to pick up her folded clothes, the moment the muscles in her back shift beneath her skin. I should be analyzing the footage for threats, for risk. That's what I'm supposed to be doing. But I'm not.

I shift in my seat to get more comfortable. The tension in my groin is making it harder to ignore the way my body reacts. Her back is bare as she moves through the room, and there's nothing practiced or artificial about it. She doesn't pose or perform. She just undresses and relaxes because she believes she's alone and safe. She's stunning without trying, and I feel it everywhere. I press play again, letting the footage run without interruption, and this time, I don't bother pretending it's for surveillance.

7

ALESSIA

The lab is quieter at night and there's less of a chance of running into Dr. Bernardi. The exam room is dim, the corridor outside sterile and empty, and the usual clatter of gurneys and low voices has gone still for the evening. There are no colleagues hovering with questions I don't want to answer. I keep my breath measured as I run the toxicology panel for the third time, eyes fixed on the monitor while the machine cycles through its process.

I lean over the workstation, scanning the readout as the results render line by line. The screen blinks to life, and I see the same readout again —trace quantities of a sedative compound I haven't seen in years. I keep telling myself something is off, but I keep getting the same results.

"That can't be right," I murmur, narrowing my eyes. I press my fingertips into the edge of the counter, grounding myself as the data continues to blink on the screen. I've rerun the sample three times now, and I can't believe what I'm seeing.

I cross-reference it with the old database I keep buried on my NAS. The compound matches the entry in my archived files. It's listed under several aliases but always flagged for restricted use. I remember it showing up once in a case review Bernardi supervised—it wasn't mine, and I was never briefed on its origin. I don't know who manufactures it or how it circulates, only that it's extremely uncommon and not something anyone uses lightly.

My father banned it years ago, said it left a trail. It was one of the last vile conversations I overheard from him before I ghosted the entire family and went my own way. I should not be seeing what I'm seeing, and I should not be put in this position. I told him to pretend I was dead, and instead, he is haunting my waking hours.

If Matteo had it in his system, someone broke protocol—or maybe it was him. Maybe my father gave the order and changed his mind, or someone else in his inner circle acted without his knowledge. The uncertainty twists in my gut as I try to reconcile what I know of him with what I'm seeing in front of me.

I pace the length of the lab, arms folded tightly. The light casts a sterile wash across the counters and floor that makes everything feel cold and sterile, but I feel dirty. My skin itches with unease.

I grab my phone and scroll to Chiara's name. It rings thrice before she picks up, and I feel better as soon as I hear her voice.

"You're up late," she answers, her voice light. I hear her shuffle something in the background—probably the stack of books she keeps by her bed.

I settle onto a stool at the counter with a huff. "I found something. In the tox panel on this autopsy I'm doing..." I grab a pen and start scribbling on the margin of a file folder already filled with notes. It gives my hands something to do while I'm nervous.

There's a pause, and when she speaks again, her tone softens. "What do you need from me?" Chiara's voice flattens, but I hear her shifting, likely sitting upright now.

"If I send you something, can you help me identify it? Or really... confirm that I'm correct?" I pin the phone tighter to my ear with my shoulder and glance down at the printed tox reports, the numbers swimming slightly as my thoughts race. Rubbing the back of my neck, I feel the faint stiffness from how long I've been hunched over my work. "It's a sedative."

"What kind of sedative?" Chiara's voice sharpens slightly, and I know she's more awake. I feel bad for disrupting her sleep.

"M99. It's not on the market. It's controlled use, and I think it links back to some organized crime." I lean back, tasting the sour words as I speak them, because the deeper truth behind them is one I don't want to face. One I don't really want her to know about me. Chiara knows nothing about my connection to the Costas and I'd like to keep it that way.

"That sounds serious," Chiara says slowly. I can hear the shift in her tone—still cautious, but more grounded now. "You know I'll help however I can. But promise me you'll be careful. That shit is used by some pretty sketchy people. Whoever the stiff is, it could be dangerous."

"I will," I say, though I'm not sure I believe it myself. "I just... I can't let this go. Something about it is eating away at me."

"I'm not asking you to let it go," she says gently. "Just don't do it alone. If you're seeing something, talk to someone who can actually help you —not just me. Isn't Dr. Bernardi good at this stuff?"

"There's no one else I trust," I admit, and I bristle at her suggestion. Bernardi would be the first person I would go to, except the way he already thinks I'm hiding stuff creeps me out. And if he knows I have a personal connection to the victim, all my work will be thrown out. Someone else will be put on this case, and that Mafia badass who keeps following me will get up close and personal really quickly.

"Well, it's gonna eat you alive. Just hand it over to that nerdy tech."

I press my fingers against my temple, the tension creeping higher. "It already is."

She's quiet for a beat, then asks, "Do you want me to come over?"

I think about it for a minute and decide it's not what I want. Maybe a glass of wine and a hot bath, not more questions and skepticism or lectures. "No," I say. "Just talking to you helps. I just needed to say it out loud."

"Then I'm here. Anytime. And Alessia?"

"Yeah?" I ask, feeling slightly better now and more ready to go home and try to sleep off this new revelation.

"Go get some sleep. Or at least lie down." I smile at her gentle mothering attempt.

"You too. 'Night."

"'Night."

We hang up without saying goodbye. I scrub my hands over my face and clean up the lab. Nothing's changed, really, except now the knot in my stomach has a name—M99.

The walk home is short but tense thanks to my handsome shadow I can basically count on at this point. My nerves buzz the entire way because I am terrified he's going to corner me and ask me what I learned today.

The hallway is quiet when I reach my floor, but the instant I reach for my keys, I feel a sliver of fear crawl down my back. The lock is scuffed. The metal casing is dented just slightly, like someone tried to force it with a tool and then gave up. I shudder and run my finger along the edge.

Someone has been here, trying to get into my apartment, and it happened sometime today. I swear that damage wasn't here when I left this morning.

I slide my phone out and type a quick message to Chiara to let her know I'm home safe, but I'm glancing over my shoulder as I do it, praying whoever it was is gone.

Alessia: 11:42 PM: Home. Talk tomorrow. Buona notte.

I don't wait for a reply from her because standing in this hallway feels too exposed. So I unlock the door, step inside, and reset the deadbolt. Then I reach for the drawer beside the fridge and pull out the small pistol I keep there. My hand doesn't shake, but my pulse jumps as I walk from room to room making sure I'm alone.

I check the rooms one by one—bathroom, bedroom, closet. Nothing's out of place, but something is off, or maybe I'm just too afraid now.

I stand in the center of the kitchen with the gun in my hand, shifting my weight from foot to foot, trying to decide whether I'm overreacting or not. I don't like feeling cornered in my own apartment, but something about the lock tells me I'm not imagining how dangerous the situation I'm in is. I grip the pistol tighter and stare at the door, trying to decide whether it's safe to stay here.

There's a knock at the door. The two solid taps are evenly spaced and controlled, with no panic or haste behind them.

I stand completely still with a rigid back and my hand tight on the gun's grip. The apartment is silent, and I listen for any follow-up sound—a footstep, a breath, anything at all—but nothing comes.

A few seconds pass. Then another knock comes, this time followed by a voice.

"Alessia." The voice is muffled but familiar. My shoulders tense as I walk closer to the door and rise up on my tiptoes to peek through the peephole.

I let a gust of air burst from my lungs—an exasperated sigh. I don't think for a second that Vinny was the one who tried breaking in. He's better than that. He'd be able to pick the lock and let himself in without my knowing it. I can almost bet on it. But I don't feel safe in here right now, and he's here...

I unlock the door but leave the chain on. "What do you want?" I keep my stance tight, fingers curled around the inner door handle, my body angled to slam it shut if I need to.

"Someone was outside when we walked up," he says. "They ran when I turned the corner. I checked the perimeter, but they're gone." He keeps his voice level, but I catch the flicker of something colder in his eyes—calculation, or maybe restraint. "I just wanted to make sure you're okay."

"Convenient," I mumble, then I narrow my eyes through the gap in the door, my pulse climbing as I scan his face for the smallest sign of dishonesty. My belly flutters as I remember the way he touched me the other night and I think about why he's even in my life right now. My father would never send one of his men in to keep an eye on me if he thought they'd harm me in any way. I know at least that much about my father is civil.

He does care, even if it's messed up the way he shows it.

Vinny meets my gaze evenly. "I'm not here to start something. I just wanted to make sure you were alright," he repeats. His stance doesn't shift, hands loose at his sides, like he knows exactly how much space to take up to avoid being threatening. I shake my head and sigh.

"You're watching me now too?" I ask as I eye the chain. The gun in my hand feels like dead weight now.

"Yes. That's the job." His reply comes fast like a well-trained soldier's response.

I close the door again and hesitate, then unhook the chain and open the door wide. My shoulders are slumped in defeat as I say, "Come in." I step aside with hesitation still prickling my spine, but knowing my father sent him gives me a bit of reassurance. A violent friend is better than an unknown enemy. If he's here to protect me from whoever it is my father thinks may come after me because of this case, he can do his job better from in here.

He steps inside without comment. I close the door behind him, relock it, and place the gun back in the drawer. His eyes follow the motion, then sweep across the entire room before landing on me again.

"You always keep that loaded?" His voice is quieter now, gaze dropping to the drawer as I close it with a firm hand.

"Always. You know who my father is." I turn back toward him slowly, letting the implication land where it needs to.

He nods like that makes perfect sense, which only pisses me off. I don't need further confirmation about why he's here or what my father asked of him.

I could be rude and park him on the sofa while I go shower, but I decide it's only polite to offer him a drink. So I walk to the fridge and pull out a bottle of chilled wine, then snag two glasses and fill them. "If someone wanted to scare me, it worked." I keep my tone flat, even as I lift the cold rim of the glass to my lips while extending the second to him.

"You think that was the goal?" He tilts his head slightly, watching me with a stillness that makes me feel seen and cornered all at once. As he takes the glass, his fingers brush over mine and again, I remember the delicate way he touched me. It makes me cradle my cheek unconsciously, and his eyes trace the movement.

"No. I think they wanted in and failed. They just didn't expect me to notice." I lower the glass to the counter and lean back, crossing my arms over my chest while I watch him sip his wine.

He folds his arms and leans against the wall. It makes his biceps push out under the tight-fitting shirt and my eyes threaten to bulge in my head. "Your father would never allow anyone to hurt you." He says it like a fact, not for comfort, and I catch myself before I snort with laughter.

I nod. "I know." I exhale slowly and blow away the frustration of that admission.

"And I wouldn't let it happen either." His gaze doesn't shift from mine, and it catches my attention. I study him carefully for a moment, noticing a softness in his expression that wasn't there before. "Whatever else I am, I'm not your enemy." He leans forward just slightly, enough to close some of the space but not all of it.

"Not yet." I say it without heat, but not without warning, letting it hang between us like a challenge.

He gives a short, humorless smile. "Fair." His mouth twitches, the closest thing I've seen to a smile that wasn't tactical.

I sip the wine again and stare at the edge of the counter. There's something about him that throws me off balance. He watches everything, says little, and yet I don't actually feel like he's spying on or stalking me.

"You can sit if you want," I say, motioning to the chair across the room. I keep my tone neutral and my posture relaxed, though my pulse hasn't slowed since he arrived.

He pulls it out and drops into it, forearms resting on the table. "You reran the tox screen." He doesn't ask it like a question. He already knows the answer and is only testing how much I'll admit. I drop into the chair next to him, unaware of how close it really is until our knees brush and he notices it.

I lift my chin as I take another swig and ask, "How do you know that?"

"Because you want answers, Alessia." He folds his hands together on the table next to where he sets his wine.

"And what do you think I found?" I keep my gaze on him, watching for the smallest flicker of reaction across his face.

He doesn't answer. I let the question hang between us, unfinished. I'm not about to divulge my secrets, but I'm not foolish enough to think men like him can't access some of them.

It's late. My limbs ache. The weight of everything I've uncovered presses hard against my skull, but I don't ask him to leave because deep down, I feel safer knowing he's here, even if my father did send him.

He doesn't offer to go, either—probably creepy under normal circumstances, and Chiari would smack me silly, but I want him here. I want to sleep tonight.

Whatever tension remains between us isn't sharp. It doesn't come with teeth. It hums beneath the quiet like something waiting to be acknowledged.

"I'm going to shower. You can help yourself to more wine." Standing, I slurp the rest of my glass and leave it on the counter. "And there are a pillow and blanket in the hallway closet, but you probably know that, don't you?"

My question is meant to bait him into admitting he was the one who was in my apartment, but he just lowers his chin and looks up at me through hooded eyes as I walk away, leaving me to wonder if I'm going insane.

At least I'll feel safe enough to sleep. That's what I have to keep telling myself.

8

VINCENZO

I pour another half glass of wine and carry it with me down the hall, feet silent on the hardwood. I think about the man I've become in the years I've worked this life—how easily I follow people, get into their homes, learn their habits, and justify all of it as protection. Alessia isn't stupid. She knew I wasn't just checking on her, but she let me in anyway. Not because she trusted me, but because she calculated the risk and made peace with it. That says more about her than it does about me.

I open the linen closet and grab a pillow, then the folded throw blanket from the top shelf. It still smells faintly like her laundry detergent she uses which I smell on her every time I've been near her. I barely register the thought before I shake it off and close the door.

Then she screams.

The wine slips from my hand and hits the floor, the glass bouncing once before rolling under the radiator. I draw my weapon and run. Her bedroom door is cracked, and I don't bother knocking. I shove it open, gun up, and race in.

Alessia's halfway undressed—bra, panties, nothing else—and she spins around in shock, eyes wild. Steam is curling from the adjoining bathroom, the light behind her backlit like a halo I have no business seeing.

"Jesus, Vinny!" she shouts, backing against the dresser. "What the hell are you doing with your gun?" Her eyes flick to the weapon, then back to me, her chest rising and falling like she's ready to throw something at my head.

"You screamed," I growl, but I don't lower the weapon until I'm sure we're alone in the room and whatever threat was there is gone. I scan the room, then the window.

The pane is cracked. Not shattered, but fractured at the base, just along the latch where someone tried to force it. I walk past her and lean in to inspect it. The lock is bent. Tools were used recently. Whoever tried this knew what they were doing, but they look out of practice.

She grabs her robe from the bed and yanks it on, glaring at me. "You think busting into my bedroom while I'm half-naked is going to help?" She tugs her robe tighter around herself and shoots me a look that could cut glass.

I holster the gun but don't step back. "Whoever tried this wasn't guessing. They wanted in." I run my fingers along the bent metal, checking for fresh marks, trying to keep my focus off the way she's glaring at me in nothing but a robe. It makes my pulse tick up a few notches and my body is responding to the bits of bare skin that are still exposed. All I can think about is watching her undress and climb into bed on that monitor the other day.

"Right," she snaps. "Or you staged it. Another scare tactic to get me to keep my mouth shut." She crosses her arms, eyes locked on mine with sharp suspicion.

I meet her glare head-on. "If I wanted you silent, you'd be gone before anyone noticed." I don't raise my voice, but the air shifts slightly between us.

The room crackles with tension, and heat, the proximity. Her robe slips slightly from one shoulder. She doesn't fix it. I let my eyes indulge for a moment before wresting them away to catch her glare.

"Is that what this is? You're inept at getting a woman so you stalk me? Did my father even send you?" Alessia moves around the foot of her bed and toward the door to the bathroom, and I watch her.

"Think what you want, but I'm here to help." And apparently, I'm here to get a very hard cock that will be very upset when it learns she wants nothing to do with me. She's furious as she walks into her bathroom, and I hear the water shut off.

I busy myself by inspecting the window again, which will have to be fixed or she won't be safe here. I may need to up the security too or we'll have a mess on our hands. If Emilio thinks it's bad now, wait until someone kills Gordo's daughter.

Alessia walks back into the room huffing and sighing in an overly dramatic fashion. It's like she is looking for a reason to be angry and blow off steam but she doesn't know how to be angry or take it out on me personally.

She crosses her arms. "Vinny. Seriously?" She plants a hand on her hip, the edge in her voice clashing with the curve of her mouth like she's trying not to smile.

I arch a brow. "What?" I lift one brow, more amused than offended.

"Vinny is a stupid name." She says it flatly, but I can tell she's baiting me.

That gets a laugh out of me. "My friends call me Enzo," I say casually, but I watch her face for a reaction anyway. It's definitely my invitation to her, but she is still being snippy.

"You don't have friends." She steps closer, and the fire in her voice feels less like an insult, more like a challenge.

"You don't think so?" I shrug and shift my stance slightly, feeling the floor under my boots like I'm about to step into something I can't walk back from. And maybe I want to. Everything about this situation is a giant red flag, and I'm barreling toward the cliff with no parachute.

She steps closer, now with both hands on her hips, and lifts one eyebrow at me. "You're the most infuriating man I've ever met," she snaps.

"You should get out more," I shoot back, crossing my arms just to keep from reaching for her.

"You're smug, you're evasive, and you're watching me like you're doing me a favor just by being here." Her nostrils flare, and I think it's cute.

"I'm here because someone tried to break in," I say. "Forgive me for not smiling about it."

"Forgive me for not wanting to be babysat by a guy with a superiority complex." Her eyes roll, and I snort in laughter.

"I never once said I was better than you, woman…" Her accusation pricks my ego, but I try to laugh it off. She wants to rile me for some reason, and it's beginning to work as she steps closer. Just not the way she thinks it is.

"You don't have to. You walk around like you're God's gift to women." Alessia's hand waves in the air, almost hitting me, and I catch her wrist and grip it hard, holding her gaze.

"You walk around like you're invincible, but you're walking on glass floors." My grip is tight but not enough to even leave a mark, and she twists her wrist to get free.

She laughs—short, sharp, annoyed. "You know what, Vinny—"

"Enzo," I say quietly.

She opens her mouth to argue again, but it doesn't happen. Her breath catches. Her hand is halfway raised like she's going to smack my face. Instead, she grabs my collar and pulls me in. Her mouth crashes into mine before either of us can say another word.

I let go of her wrist and grab her by the waist, pulling her flush to me as her hands fist in the collar of my shirt. She tastes like wine, but the intoxicating part is how her tongue traces the line of my lip while I crush her to my body and grind my hard dick into her belly.

She breaks the kiss first, breathing hard. Her robe has slipped completely open and the towel is in a puddle around her feet.

I rest my forehead against hers. "You really think I staged it?" I keep my forehead against hers, watching her eyes flick from my mouth to the broken window and back again.

She doesn't answer, but she does unhook her bra, and a lump forms in my throat. She kisses me again, and this time, both of her hands are on the lapels of my jacket, pulling me forward as she backs toward her bed.

Her mouth is more insistent, her need palpable as she presses against me. I don't hesitate to lift her up and carry her over to the bed, letting her legs wrap around my waist. Her kisses taste of desperation and desire, as if she's been trying to forget me just as much as I have her. It's like feeding an addiction I never knew I had until now.

My hands roam over her body, learning every curve and contour under the thin fabric of her robe. I can feel her heat through the silk, and it only fuels my growing hunger for her. Her skin is so soft, so warm, and I can't get enough.

"Enzo," she whimpers, arching her back and exposing the beautiful expanse of her neck. I growl low in response, my grip on her hips tightening as our kisses intensify. Greedily, I pepper her collarbone with open-mouthed kisses, trailing heat in their wake.

As I peel back the edge of her robe, the culmination of my every fantasy is laid bare before me. Her breasts are perfect—round and firm, capped with hardened nipples that beg for my attention. She lies on the bed with her hair splayed wildly around her face as I rip off my jacket and then my shirt. Her hands reach for the fly of my slacks, and I let her undo them and pull my hard dick out.

She wraps her fingers around my length, stroking me to full attention as I groan in pleasure. Her hand continues to work my length as I push my pants down and toe off my shoes before crawling over her, finally breaking her grip on me.

"You're so damn hot, Alessia," I growl against her skin. I suddenly need more of her, to have every inch of our bodies pressed together. I kick the pants off and hook my fingers around the elastic of her black silky panties and pull them until she shimmies her legs out and is spread for me.

I skim my hand down her stomach, causing gooseflesh to rise in its wake. Her breath hitches as I reach between her legs, brushing over her damp folds. She's wet and hot for me, and it sends a jolt straight to my cock. "You're soaked," I whisper, nipping at her earlobe before biting it lightly.

Her hips buck at my touch as I rub her clit and spread the moisture. What I wouldn't do to have this little minx tied up as my fuck toy all night long, but if wind got back to Gordo, I'd never hear the end of it. I have to let her lead.

"Fuck me..." she breathes, and I get the feeling this isn't the wine talking.

"So impatient, *Bella*," I tease, but I can't blame her. Her scent is driving me wild, and I need her just as much. I run my fingertips over her heated folds, delving just the tip of my finger inside her slick entrance. She whimpers, arching her hips upward, silently begging for more.

I brush my lips against hers. "You taste so good, Alessia," I moan, wanting to savor every inch of her. "And you feel even better."

Her nails dig into my back as I trace a leisurely path over her swollen nub, down to her entrance and beyond, then back up. I can feel her quivering beneath me, anticipating where my mouth is going next. "Enzo," she moans, and it's the sexiest thing I've ever heard. It sets my blood on fire.

I freeze at her moan, my cock throbbing with need as I look up at her face. Her eyes are closed, a flush creeping up her cheeks, and she bites her lip in pleasure. I want more of that sound. More of her.

I shift between her legs, my engorged cock aching for her. Holding her gaze, I tease the tip against her wet entrance, letting us both feel the electricity between us. I watch as realization dawns in her expressive eyes—this time, there's no denying the lust between us.

"Fuck," I growl, unable to take it anymore. With sheer willpower, I enter her slowly, inch by achingly slow inch. Her walls grip me tightly, rippling around me in pleasure and welcome. She grunts and arches off the bed as I bottom out and start thrusting.

Her wetness coats us, our bodies moving together in a rhythm that feels like we were made for each other. "Fuck, you feel so good," she moans, and it's like gasoline on an already raging inferno.

I reach to cup her breast, rolling the aching peak between my thumb and forefinger as I continue my relentless pace. Her eyes fly open in surprise before rolling back in ecstasy. "Oh, fuck, yes," she moans, her toes curling in pleasure. "More."

With a growl of hunger and need, I increase my pace, taking her harder, deeper. I want to be deep inside her forever, marking her as mine. My gaze locks with hers as we move together, our bodies in tune with each other's rhythm as if we've always known this moment would come.

I slip a hand between her thighs, finding her wet and aching for me. My cock throbs, but I hold back, teasing her swollen clit with the pad of my finger as I continue moving inside her. A whimper escapes her lips as she bites down on her bottom lip. "Enzo... More..."

"You like that, do you?" I say in her ear, relishing in her surrender.

"God, yes," she moans, arching her back and inviting me deeper into her tight heat. As much as I want to please her, I can't help but feel possessive, territorial. She is mine tonight... and maybe more if I play my cards right.

Alessia's nails dig into my shoulders, leaving bloody trails as she writhes beneath me.

I'm losing control, her tight heat milking me with every thrust, and her low moans of pleasure are the sweetest music to my ears. "Bella," I growl, my voice a deep rumble as I thrust deeper, harder. She's so wet, so tight, and all around perfect. I don't ever want to let go.

"I..." She grunts, and I feel it before she can even express it. Her pussy clamps down hard on my dick, making it impossible to thrust into her. She's so tight I have to be deliberate about the way I fuck her, and it sends me toppling over the edge.

Ecstasy washes over me, and I'm powerless against it. Her name is on my lips as I empty everything I have into her, collapsing atop her sweat-slicked form. My heartbeat races in my ears, and hers too, crashing against mine in an erratic rhythm that slowly starts to even out.

"Holy shit," she pants, and I can only manage a nod in agreement as I catch my breath. Slowly, I realize my weight is on top of her and roll to the side, pulling her with me so we rest on our sides. My hand idly strokes her hip as my heart rate returns to normal, but the rush of adrenaline is long gone. All that remains are a sated exhaustion and lingering lust in my veins.

Alessia curls into me softly, and I hold her, pressing a kiss to the back of her shoulder. She says nothing, which says more than she thinks it does, and when I start to pull away, she grips my wrist and brings it back over her body. So I shift, pulling the covers up over us, and lie next to her, staring at the ceiling as she starts to fall asleep.

Lots of things have happened when I was put on a mark before, but fucking them isn't one of them. I've crossed a line I can't uncross, but I can't say I'm apologetic about it.

Gordo will be pissed.

Emilio won't understand.

But what's done is done.

Now I have to convince her to let me keep her safe or whoever tried to break in here today might just get what they want.

9

ALESSIA

I wake to cold sheets and the sound of the radiator knocking through the apartment. Enzo's side of the bed is empty. No note, no message. Just the faintest dent in the pillow where his head had been and the lingering scent of his cologne.

I force myself to get out of bed when I really want to lie here and stew over what happened and what it means. The heat of the shower helps me shake it off a little, but what really does it is the brisk walk across town.

By the time I get to the lab, the day's already off to a bad start. The cappuccino machine is broken. The receptionist glares like I'd personally offended her. Then I open the door to my office and find Luca Bernardi leaning against my desk like he owns this whole department, though he's really just the supervisor in charge of things. Higher-ups don't rein him in, though.

He lifts a brow. "You're late." I drop my keys in the tray by the microscope, letting the clang echo through the room, and I don't bother with an apology. If he's waiting for one, he'll be disappointed.

"You're in my seat," I say flatly, tossing my bag onto the counter. I move toward him without breaking eye contact, forcing him to acknowledge my presence. He's not a bad boss, but this stiff we've been working on seems to have brought out some dark streak in him that butts heads with what my father expects of me.

He stays where he is, deliberately, so I have to physically walk around him to get a different chair. His button-down shirt is loose at the collar, and his lab coat is nowhere in sight, giving him the air of someone who thinks the rules only apply to his subordinates, not him. The smile on his face is slow and practiced, but it doesn't touch his eyes. Creepy.

"Heard you've been putting in long nights," Luca says, idly thumbing through the stack of case files I left on my desk. "Stressful week?" He lifts a file and flips it open like he's reading for sport, not substance. His fingers leave faint smudges on the corner of the folder, and it makes my skin itch.

I fold my arms. "Do you need something from me, sir?" My tone cuts sharper than intended, and I see the way his jaw tightens. The muscles in his neck flex like he's holding something back.

He looks up at me from the file, eyes sharp now. "The task force has questions. *Polizia* are waiting. They're impatient for answers, and they think you're holding out." He sets the file down slowly, watching my reaction like he's measuring my pulse and breath.

I stare at him as the tension starts to swirl in my chest. I can't really read him right now, which I'm normally good at, but fucking Enzo last night got in my head. I don't know which way is up. "Are you threatening me?" I don't flinch, not even when he shifts his weight like he might move closer. My spine locks straight.

He clicks his tongue. "Friendly warning. You look tired. You should rest more." He gestures lazily toward my chair, like he's doing me a favor by keeping it warm. The arrogance in that movement makes my stomach turn.

BEAUTIFUL EVIDENCE

"I need space to do my work," I say, looking down at my desk so I don't have to look him in the eye anymore. The air between us snaps taut, and I catch the flicker in his eyes before he schools his expression. It's confirmation enough that he has a burr up his ass about me for some reason. He takes a step forward, suddenly all business.

"Enough excuses. We need results," he says, voice clipped. "Get the rest of those samples tested today and finalize your report. The task force wants movement before this case goes cold, and I won't have them thinking my lab's dragging its feet." He waits a beat to let it sink in, then he stands and turns toward the door like the matter's settled.

I hold his gaze a second longer, then sit down before I do something crazy like smack him. "Please leave my office." I point to the hallway like I'm dismissing a technician, not my boss. My hand trembles slightly, but I keep it steady.

He goes, but not before flashing that same thin smile that says he knows more than he's telling me. The door swings shut behind him, and I heave out a sigh of frustration, driving my elbows into my desk and covering my face. I'm being squeezed from both sides—Enzo who wants me to bury evidence, no doubt, and Bernardi who just wants me to do my job, get the truth.

Neither of them is giving me room to breathe. One man wants loyalty. The other demands results, and I'm trapped trying to serve both without losing myself in the process. I feel like a live wire strung between two power lines—ready to snap. There's no middle ground. No one to trust. And every time I think I've found my footing, someone moves the line again. I hate the feeling that no matter which way I lean, I'm betraying someone.

The rest of the day grinds by and nothing lines up. These case files feel heavier the longer I stare at them. I keep thinking back to what Dr. Bernardi didn't say—what he hinted at. When the word "task force" slipped out, I knew what he meant. They're not just looking for a killer. They're trying to build a larger case—*Article 416-bis: Criminal*

Association with Mafia Ties. If I get it wrong, the whole investigation could collapse.

But if I do what Bernardi wants, I personally sentence my father to a life in prison and probably men associated with him too—like Vincenzo. Like Uncle Emilio...

I leave work feeling so heavy I want to collapse. By the time I get home, my feet ache and there's a tight pulse blooming behind my eyes. I kick off my shoes and rub at my temples, but the pressure doesn't let up. The apartment feels too quiet tonight. Like he was never here.

Maybe I should be relieved, because I did, after all, run away from my legacy and my father's name. Until Enzo stormed into my life and that stiff landed on my table, I was Alessia Leone, star medical examiner. Not Alessia Costa, daughter of a Mafia hit man. I left that world behind when I changed my name, and Enzo sleeping in my bed threatens to suck me back into that black hole I escaped.

I don't bother with a glass. I pour the last inch of scotch down my throat in one gulp and sit at the kitchen table, staring at the grains of the wood. My eyes trace each line, following the swirling pattern like a maze. My fingers drum against the base of the bottle in a slow, steady pattern, a metronome for my thoughts.

My phone buzzes with an encrypted number—one I've memorized but never saved, though I've always known it would come back. It's the only tie left, but I can't bear to break it even though I know what it means. The sound cuts through the room, and a jolt runs through me like a spark of static, making me jump.

"Hello?" I answer. My voice comes out steadier than I feel. I brace myself against the table with one hand, the other gripping the phone like I might drop it. These calls always scare the fuck out of me, and it's not even that I fear him. I am not afraid of my father at all. I'm afraid of what my future means if he's in it.

My father's voice comes through, tight and low. "Alessia, *Tesoro*. Stop digging, *figlia mia*." The way he says my name makes my throat constrict. I hear the emotion in his tone, the way he cares for me. I've never doubted he loves me. But there's a rasp there I haven't heard before.

I sit up straighter. "Where are you?" I stand without realizing it, pacing now with short, sharp steps. The walls feel like they're leaning inward at me, trying to collapse the life I've built for myself, and all he had to do was call to make it happen.

"It doesn't matter, Lessi. The more you know, the worse this gets. I tried to keep you out of this." There's frustration behind his words and a tiredness that feels like he's weighing how much to tell me. Like maybe he's depending on me in ways he knows I can't offer him.

Leaning on the bar, I rub my forehead and sigh. "Then why send Vincenzo? Why pretend you're protecting me?" My voice cracks at the edges and I wish I hadn't drunk all of that scotch.

"I didn't send him. That was Emilio, *figlia mia*. You weren't supposed to get this close. I swear I told him to stay out of it." He exhales heavily, like the admission costs him something, and each word drips with resignation.

"Close to what? To the truth? To what you did to Vescari?" I straighten and stare at the dark window, seeing nothing. The city's lights blur behind my reflection, but I know he's out there somewhere, hiding away in some hole he dug to avoid being responsible and doing the right thing.

He digs his heels in with an attitude I know well. "Not everything is what it seems. Let it go." His words slap me the way they used to when I was younger. He never had to lay a hand on me because I knew not to anger him. He's already decided that I'm going to play along with him and this is some sort of warning shot.

I pause, listening. There's noise in the background—horns, traffic, someone yelling in a dialect that isn't Roman. Footsteps echo off stone.

"You're not in Rome. Where are you?" I press the phone tighter to my ear, straining for any detail. My heart kicks once, hard.

He doesn't answer.

"*Papà*—" I barely get the word out before the click ends the call. It slices the air—and my heart—like a blade.

The line goes dead. My hand stays frozen at my ear, phone pressed tight like I can will the connection back into existence. But he's long gone like a ghost in darkness, and I have more questions than answers now. He knows I'll find things, and he's scared I will use them.

I stand there for a long time with the phone still in my hand. The air in my apartment feels thicker and harder to breathe in, but it's all in my head. I know Vincenzo is sitting outside in his van watching—him or one of his men—and no one is getting at me without his seeing it. And I know my father won't hurt me, but that doesn't mean others won't try.

When I finally breathe, it comes out shallow. I dig through my cupboards in hopes to find any bottle of wine or whiskey and come up empty, so I resign myself to the fact that sleep will come hard tonight.

Then I lock every door, double-check the windows, and sit on the edge of the bed with the lights still on. My spine doesn't relax, even when I try.

It's not my father's warning that scares me. It's that he called at all. And that he's running too.

10

VINCENZO

The man waiting in the alley keeps checking his watch like he's late for something. He's wiry and jumpy, with eyes that never stop scanning the space around him. Informants like this don't last long—not because someone gets to them, but because they always think someone will. Fear turns your brain to mush over time, and this one looks particularly susceptible to it.

I light a cigarette and lean against the wall across from him. Let him come to me. I have time—not all day, but I'm not in a rush or anything. The information I need is more important than rushing it out of him and getting lies or fear-laced facts that are half-baked and unhelpful.

He walks over to me after a minute. His eyes still flick nervously up the alley, but he's making his move at least. "It wasn't sanctioned," he says, shifting from foot to foot like he's afraid the ground might open up beneath him. He's terrified of me, and he's right to be. If he lies to me, I'll kill him.

"Vescari?" I keep my voice level, but my eyes lock on his as I take a drag of my cigarette. When Emilio told me someone called to say they had information for me, I thought I'd be meeting some dark figure. This half-wit is probably a hired hand, someone still in training for whatever position they're seeking, and by the looks of it, he's failing.

He nods, tugging the hood of his sweatshirt higher like he thinks it'll hide his face. "They moved him to a secondary location. It wasn't the police, and it wasn't his family." He rubs the back of his neck, glancing over his shoulder like he's being followed. He's telling me shit I already know, except for the secondary location bit. That's new.

"Drugs?" I narrow my eyes and take a step closer, watching for the twitch in his answer as I flick ash from my burning cigarette.

"Probably—there aren't a lot of details, man." His voice dips, and he hunches his shoulders, turning to check the alley again. He's too jumpy. He'll never make it out here.

I grind the cash under my boot. "And you don't know who did it." I take another drag and eye him, skeptical that he's even sober. He seems to be tweaking or something.

"I know nothin', dude. Vescari was moved. That's all I'm saying." He glances at me, then away, like he regrets opening his mouth at all. Then he leans in. "If I had to guess—off the record—it wasn't a hit. And it sure as hell wasn't Bianchi-sanctioned. I'd say it was a crime of passion. Someone fucked him up bad and then tried to make it look like it wasn't them." His voice drops to a whisper, and he inches back into the shadow of the wall.

My jaw tightens. "So someone moved him without permission, questioned him off-book, and now he's dead." I let the words settle, watching his reaction more than listening for a reply.

He nods. "And you're asking the wrong questions if you're only looking at the body." He backs away a step, already trying to disappear into the alley. "You gotta check all the Costa safehouses, man."

I toss more cigarette ash at him, crush it, then walk away, and he doesn't follow. Smart. The last thing I need right now is to have to clean up my own crime scene. If he thinks checking Emilio's safehouses is the way to get more answers, he knows more than he's letting on—or the people who sent him with intel know more.

I slide into the car, kill the rest of the cigarette in the ashtray, and pull into traffic. The informant's words echo as I head toward Emilio's office, engine humming. I don't know what I expect to hear when I tell him, but I know he won't like knowing Gordo had the balls to interrogate Vescari and beat him, then move him and murder him. One cleanup location is bad enough, but two means more work. If we can even find it.

Emilio's pacing. That's how I know he's not in the mood to hear anything I have to say, but I say it anyway because he pays me to get to the bottom of things. When I walk in, he stops and stares up at me. His white suit is crumpled from being worn all day, and his eyes have sleep circles under them.

"He was held somewhere else before he died. Drugged, maybe, but it wasn't his family." I speak evenly, watching Emilio's every move as I deliver the news.

He stops pacing and turns. "Who did it?" He stops in his tracks and stares at me like I might pull a name out of my pocket like a fucking rabbit, but I don't have all the answers yet. He's on edge, and I understand why. He's trying to prove it was his brother to ease his mind as to why Gordo vanished, and he needs to protect himself in the event that the authorities piece together enough evidence.

"The informant didn't know, but he's sure it wasn't someone in our ranks fucking up. And it wasn't the Bianchis." I cross my arms and lean against the wall, letting him stew on it. "It's Gordo, man. You have to let me work this the right way, Boss. If the *polizia* get their hands on a bad report, it'll lead to a 416-bis. You know if that happens, we all go under. No hired hand in the entire country will be able to dissolve that much evidence."

Emilio mutters something under his breath then grumbles, "Luca Bernardi. That little shit's too close to this. We act now." Emilio slams his palm on the desk, rattling a half-empty glass of grappa.

"We can't," I say, holding his gaze and refusing to flinch. "Not yet." I keep my tone calm, steady. Someone has to be. I'm shaking my head at him because he's too impulsive. This is why his son needs to take over already. Someone has to rein in his impulsivity.

"The 416-bis case is gaining ground. We don't have time to wait." He starts pacing again, one hand gripping the back of his neck. I can see the way his eyes bulge and know he's angry and losing touch on reality.

"And if we kill him now, we hand Greco a martyr," I counter, stepping into his path to make him stop moving and listen. "We hold any more activity until we see the Bianchi response. I've got it under control, Boss. Let me deal with Alessia." I let the name hang there, watching the effect it has on him.

"You can't let this go to trial. I know she's my niece, but if killing her is the only way to keep things silent—"

"No," I say firmly. "If we kill her, they will double down. They'll look into her death and see she's connected, and it gives them more proof. We wait and pressure her to do the right thing for us."

"And if she doesn't?" he asks, narrowing his eyes. I can see the fury behind them, but he is leaning into my logic at this point.

"She will."

After another twenty minutes of convincing him to trust me, I duck out. The heat has been turned up to roughly the temperature of the sun, and with Bernardi and Greco pushing to open their 416-bis investigation, I need to apply more of this pressure to Alessia, so that's where I go. Her lab this late is a long shot, but my guys outside her apartment say she's not come home yet.

Alessia looks up the moment I walk into the lab. Her eyes are dark with irritation—or maybe it's nerves. She doesn't ask why I'm here, but she doesn't act surprised to see me. She sets down her pen and looks up at me as I walk closer.

"Have you heard whether Bernardi is setting up a task force?" I keep my voice low, watching the twitch in her fingers. I wish it were as easy as explaining to her what it would mean if she doesn't falsify that report before it's too late, but just because someone is born to the family doesn't make them loyal. She works for enemy number one, and that makes her a liability.

"No," she says, her eyes flicking away from mine too quickly. Her response is flat and immediate, a little too fast to be convincing. She picks up the pen again and pretends to jot a note, which betrays her sense of anxiety. Rubbing the bridge of my nose, I think about how this will play out when she realizes she'll either protect us or they will kill her.

I watch her for a moment. "They'll open one soon, and things will move faster then. We can't afford noise, Alessia." Stepping closer to her, I notice her tension, the way her shoulders are tight. She's trapped in this mess by no fault of her own, and I know all she probably wants is for this to go away.

"Thanks for the update," she says, tossing her pen onto the desk. "I'll alert the press." Her sarcasm barely covers the tension in her voice.

"Don't do that," I say evenly, stepping closer so she can feel the warning in my tone. "Don't get hostile with me. I'm here to help you. I am trying to protect you." While that's only a partial truth, I mean it more today than I did over a week ago when I first told her. Fucking a woman changes the way you look at her, and there's nothing you can do to change that.

She stiffens but doesn't look up. "If you're here to intimidate me, try harder. I'm not scared of you." She turns her chair slightly, probably to avoid looking at me, but I notice how afraid she looks. I want to reach out and rub her shoulders, loosen some of that tension.

"I'm not here to scare you, Bella." I shake my head once, then take a step closer. "I'm here to tell you the only thing keeping you out of the crosshairs right now is your last name—and even that's starting to wear thin." I cross the space between us to stand behind her. She smells like a strange mix of perfume and chemicals. I brush the hair over her shoulder and let my hand linger as my knuckles brush over her cheek.

That gets her attention. Her head turns slightly as if she is looking down at my shoes and back at me. "So this is about my father." Her voice is flat, but I can see more tension climbing into her shoulders.

"Emilio knows he killed Matteo. No one's pretending otherwise." I don't sugarcoat it, and I don't blink.

She exhales through her nose, sharp and angry. "Then why am I still here? Why haven't you dragged me into the street yet? I have the proof. I ran the test. I know how this goes." Her voice quavers, but she grits her teeth firmly.

"Because I told them not to." I watch her face as I say it, not knowing how it will affect her. I let the words land. "But I can't protect you if you say the wrong thing to the wrong person. Greco wants a headline. You give it to her, and you're done. Emilio… He doesn't want…" I keep my voice low, like I'm already mourning what comes next if she fucks this up.

"You're trying to manipulate me." She pushes back from the desk, eyes locked on mine with sharp defiance as she finally turns to face me.

"No," I say, holding her gaze without blinking. "I'm trying to keep you alive." My hand rises to cup her cheek, and she averts her eyes.

"Why would they kill me?" Her bottom lip quivers as she asks the question, but I know she already knows the truth. Rats in this business aren't welcome. She's not in the business, but she knows the stakes, and that makes her cat bait.

"Alessia, trust me. I want them to back off, but the only way is if you don't tell them what you know. And we either have to change evidence or we have to burn the body." I'm in this line of work, so it comes naturally to me. But she's not. She's innocent of it all, having run away before she knew too much.

"Please leave," she says firmly, and I sigh and back away.

My time will be better spent keeping her safe from any Bianchi interest for right now. They will want the truth, but they won't want the 416-bis case opened, either. Dragging Vescari's name into this will mean the downfall of multiple Roman families, and if she doesn't play ball, she will strike out fast.

I leave her alone to process what I've said, and I don't know what she'll do. So far, her life has been left alone because Gordo put a bounty on anyone who came near her. Now, who knows?

The drive across town is quiet except for the hum of the engine and the occasional buzz of a message I ignore. My route takes me through Trastevere's back streets, narrow alleys and shuttered storefronts passing like a reel I've seen too many times. I pull up a block away from the last safe house we stopped keeping tabs on—a place even Emilio doesn't mention anymore. If Gordo kept Vescari stashed somewhere off the record, this is the most likely spot.

The house off Via Portuense is one of the family's quiet spots—unmarked, rarely used. There are no cameras on it at all and no major security. It does have a keypad lock and the kind of insulation in the walls that makes for a quieter atmosphere inside—not to block out city noise, but to keep the torture sounds inside. If Gordo was gonna do something, this would be the place.

Inside, the place smells like bleach, but the floor tells a different story. There are scuff marks across the floor and a smear of something dark near the drain in the kitchen sink that could be blood. I check the vent slats, under the sink, the seams of the windows, and find nothing. My eyes scan every surface, every corner, every shelf and cupboard. It feels like it could take hours to fully tear this place apart, but my eyes catch on something.

The socket near the back room is loose, so I walk over and pry it open with a key. Inside, I find a folded piece of paper and a burner phone with its SIM out, tucked behind exposed wires. Carefully, I pry them out while using my key fob to hold the live wires to the side. Whoever hid this shit in here wasn't messing around. I think they were hoping that someone would come looking and get a shock.

I shove both the SIM and the paper into my jacket pocket without thinking twice. If there is a call history on that SIM, I'll be able to lift it off, maybe other things too. If Gordo is smart, though, he won't have left this much proof anywhere. Still, if there's a chance it was Vescari who put this here, we can use whatever is on this to help convince Alessia to do the right thing.

Gordo bringing Vescari back to one of Emilio's safehouses wasn't just stupid, it was reckless—the first fuckup in a line of massive fuckery. If we don't bury this fast, it'll be the crack that brings the whole goddamn house down.

I head back to the car with the SIM burning a hole in my pocket. I want to dig into this and find any other loose end out there so I can tie them up and hang Bernardi's 416-bis investigation by its skinny neck and put this nightmare behind us.

11

ALESSIA

Three days pass, filled with tension and silence, each one tightening the noose around my nerves as I wait for the next shoe to drop. Enzo or one of his men follows me to and from work, to the shops, to the stylist for my haircut. I want to say I feel safe, but I don't.

Even work isn't normal. Nothing feels right anymore. The rhythm of the lab has gone slack, and everyone knows it. People speak in half-sentences around me, hushed tones, and evasive eyes. Dr. Bernardi hovers more than normal, and the morgue feels colder than usual. I'm starting to wonder if it's me or if everyone knows that I'm purposefully stalling this autopsy report to give myself time to decide what's the right thing to do.

It's dusk by the time I leave work for that night. The sky is a soft bruise, and the street lamps flicker on in patches. I start walking my normal route, but Enzo doesn't pop out to follow me. Two men are here this time, chatting with each other. And I feel safe until I've crossed Via del Corso and sense them getting closer. That prickling sensation between my shoulder blades creeps into my blood and makes my heart beat oddly.

I glance back. I don't recognize these men at all. They're not talking or checking their phones the way Enzo's men do. They're watching me. It makes me shudder, but I try to relax. He put his number into my phone, but if I take time to stop and search for his contact now, those men will definitely catch up to me.

I pivot right, then cut across the next intersection. They follow, getting closer by the second, and I get the feeling that they've done something to one of Enzo's men who was supposed to be here to protect me. This is what he means. Not protection from Bernardi or my father. Whoever these assholes are, these are the ones Enzo thinks may do me harm.

I try again—left this time, through a shuttered alley, out toward the south end of the piazza. I stop briefly at a corner stand, pretending to check my bag. They stop too. They're still there, eyes locked on me like I'm already boxed in.

My pulse kicks into overdrive. I have no weapon, no badge, and no one I trust enough to call. Rome is a huge, scary place and there are several dark places I have to walk through before I get home. My mind races with the idea that these are the men who tried getting into my apartment, broke my window.

I slip between the bakery and the old bookstore, letting the alleyway narrow behind me. My feet echo in the narrow space, damp stone reflecting back a weak draft. I cut behind the back of a boarded-up building and come out by the closed cinema. When I look again, they're gone.

They're gone, disappeared into the corners of Rome like they were never there at all.

I brace one hand against the wall, drag in a breath. I want to think I lost them. I want to force myself to believe it.

But I don't believe it for a second.

It's a two-minute walk to my Aunt Rosa's place, and I take it fast. I duck through side streets and back entrances, ignoring the sting in my calves and the burn in my lungs. By the time I reach the alley behind her apartment, I feel half-mad and half-frozen and my legs and lower back hurt from practically running in heels.

I knock twice and pause and hear men's voices coming up the sidewalk. It's hurried steps, too, and ragged breathing. They know they lost me and now they're searching and thankfully, I'm here.

The security chain slides against the metal frame, and the door opens. Rosa's eyes widen when she sees me. My heart is pounding and tears are brimming in my eyes. I'm so relieved to find her home. I've never just shown up without calling. My mother's sister has cut all ties with the Costas since Mama died, and we've barely spoken too.

"Alessia?" Her eyes scan the street behind me before she opens all the way.

"Can I come in?" My voice comes out tight, barely louder than the hum of a car passing on the street behind me.

She nods and closes the door, then unhooks the chain all the way and opens. I step inside into warmth and lavender and the faintest smell of orange rind. I've only been here a few times, but her apartment always smells like a recipe that just finished.

Her rotund frame wraps around me, and I hug her as I let out a few soft tears and sniffle into her curly wig. I don't want to let her go because I'm afraid, but I know I'm safe inside here. They won't find me, and I can try to get ahold of Enzo.

"Sit. I'll get tea." She moves toward the stove with the same purposeful grace she's always had, and I do as I'm told. The chair creaks under me, and I realize my hands are shaking as I sit and watch her bustle around the open space.

Aunt Rosa doesn't comment on my nerves. She probably assumes she knows what's going on, that this is related to my father—and she's not wrong. But she pours water into the kettle and lights the stove.

"You look like you ran here." She doesn't say it unkindly, just with that Rosa bluntness that leaves no room for pretense.

"I think I was followed," I tell her, "from the morgue. Two men. But I lost them near the south piazza." My voice is steady, but my fingers won't stop curling into the fabric of my coat. This whole thing has gotten way out of control. I could've filed the report and been done with this, but after what Enzo told me, I'm afraid to. If I lie on it, Dr. Bernardi comes after me. If I tell the truth, every scumbag in this city might.

Rosa's back straightens, and she sets down a mug in front of me and drops a tea bag into it. "Did they threaten you?" She doesn't blink as she asks, but neither do I as I answer her.

"No. They didn't have to." I shake my head and pull my coat tighter around my shoulders. "But I'm scared."

She bustles back to the kitchen as the kettle starts to whistle quietly and then comes back. After she fills my mug with hot water, she sits across from me. "Then you need to go to the authorities. Now." She leans forward and pushes the mug toward me but rests a hand on my knee.

I let out a short, humorless breath. "You think I haven't considered that? I don't even know who's watching me. It could be the Bianchis. It could be my father's people. Hell, it could be someone I haven't even thought of." I push a hand through my hair, breathing hard through my nose.

"Who can you call? Someone who can actually help you?" Rosa nudges the cup toward me again, and I sigh and pick it up.

I look away, ashamed of how this situation has gotten so messy and somewhat personal. "It's... complicated." I glance down, tracing the rim of my cup with one fingertip. I don't prefer tea. I'm more of a wine sort of girl. But I don't want to be rude, so I bring it to my lips and sip it.

"I blame your father," she says, clicking her tongue. "You need to get away from that job. I know you like it, but it's too close, *Tesora*. I know you love the science, but they can use you, manipulate you."

"I don't know what else I would do…" My voice cracks, and I hate how small it makes me sound. I press my palm against my forehead while I think.

The DNA is still inconclusive, but that's no longer what keeps me awake at night. What matters is the new timestamp on a fluid marker. Matteo had a sedative in his system, and it metabolized too slowly to have been administered right before death. Which means someone drugged him earlier. Someone held him somewhere. And that changes everything. It means it wasn't a crime of passion. It was premeditated. And if it was my father, it changes how I see him.

I take a sip of tea, mostly to buy time while I try to push the tremble out of my voice. But I can't manage to fake being okay in front of Aunt Rosa.

"Well, I'm not letting you leave alone. I'll drive you." She goes to get up, but I grab her wrist.

"No," I blurt out, because I can only imagine what these men will do to her if they see her dropping me off. They'll follow her home and use her as leverage to get to me, and I'll never forgive myself. I suck in a breath and say, "I'll call someone."

I pull out my phone and scroll to Vincenzo's number. He used "Vinny", probably as a joke since I told him it was a stupid name. I don't even know what I'm going to say, but I hit *Dial*.

He picks up on the third ring. "Leone? You okay?" His voice cuts through the line like a blade, and instead of scaring me, it makes me feel safer instantly.

"I got followed today. I was followed by two men outside of work." I stand and pace across the small kitchen, one arm wrapped around my waist. "They might've hurt your guys. I didn't see them." Enzo growls into the mic and grunts out his response.

"Are you home?" I hate how he sounds demanding, but part of me feels safer knowing he's that protective. I ignore the part where he is possessive, though.

"No. I'm at my Aunt Rosa's." I move to the window, checking the street out of habit. It's dark and I don't see any movement or strange shadows. But that doesn't mean they're not watching.

"Is the place secure?" I hear a door slam in the background on his end of the line, then I hear an engine roar to life.

I look toward the door with its single deadbolt and flimsy chain, but I answer, "Yes." I say it quietly, my fingers still curled around the phone. I force the word out and lean against the window frame, as if it can hold me up. Rosa smiles at me from where she's perched on the couch watching. I hope he hurries because I want to be out of here before they come knocking and find out I have a relative I care about.

"Stay there." It's a command, not a suggestion. Enzo hangs up on me, and the line goes silent before I turn to see Rosa's hopeful expression.

I sigh and drop the phone into my coat pocket. Rosa raises one eyebrow. "Was that him?" Rosa asks, not looking up from the stove.

"Yes," I say, walking back over to slump into the chair and pick up the tea again.

"You two don't sound like friends." She turns around and scowls at me disapprovingly, the way my mother would if she were here, but I shrug it off.

"We're not." Not friends, not lovers, not even acquaintances. He's managing my life like he owns me right now, but it isn't even by my father's direct order. I was a fool to trust him, but here we are.

Ten, maybe fifteen minutes crawl by—long enough for the tea to cool and for Rosa to start fidgeting with the hem of her blouse. Her lectures about cutting myself off from my father more completely aren't just white noise, and I've just started to think maybe he won't come when there's a knock on the door.

Rosa stiffens. Her eyes go wide as I rise and cross to the peephole. It's Vincenzo, and not a moment too soon.

I pull the door open wider and step aside. "Come in," I say gruffly. It isn't ideal to introduce Rosa to men like him, and I know what she'll think when she sees the tattoos creeping out of his collar. But he came because I called him.

Vincenzo steps inside with his usual dominant posture, scanning the apartment instinctively. Rosa stands behind me, arms crossed, eyes narrowing.

"Aunt Rosa," I say, turning to her with a breath I didn't realize I'd been holding, "this is Vincenzo Morelli. He's... helping me."

Rosa doesn't offer her hand, but she nods once. "Then he can sit, and you can both stop pretending he's just a kind, helpful stranger." She glares at me knowingly, and I tense.

My shoulders are stiff and I can't make eye contact with her due to shame. She has kept her whole life away from this and I've dragged it right to her doorstep. I didn't mean it this way. I was just afraid.

Vincenzo's expression is unreadable as he says, "Thank you."

He follows me into the living room after I lock up and lowers himself onto the edge of the chair across from me. I sit again too and pick up the tea out of nervous habit. Rosa shifts in her seat and folds her hands in front of herself as Enzo starts talking to me.

"You want to tell me about the police summons, or should I guess?" He doesn't beat around the bush at all, does he? I heave out a sigh as Rosa's eyes lift to look at me in concern.

I bite back a curse. "You have people reading my emails now?" I snap, heat flaring in my chest.

"I have people keeping you alive. Big difference." He doesn't flinch when he says it, but he does hold a calming hand out toward my aunt who has no clue what she's even overhearing right now.

"We shouldn't be talking about this now. It's not why I asked you to come." Humiliation dusts my cheeks as I set the tea I'm clearly not going to drink down and hug my arms over my belly.

"No," he says, leaning closer. "I'm here because you haven't made a decision yet." His eyes search mine like he's trying to pin me in place. I glance at Aunt Rosa nervously again, but she's staring at her hands now. I know that posture too. She's scared. She knows this could come back to bite her. I hate that I've dragged her even an inch closer to my father's world.

"About what?" I ask, though I continue flicking glances at my aunt hoping Enzo will get the point.

"Whose side you're on." His voice is unbending and rigid. He frowns and turns to Aunt Rosa, but she looks up and glares.

Rosa glares at us, waving a hand like we're school kids. "Enough. If you're going to fight, do it outside." Rosa points her spoon at us like it's a weapon. Then she sighs and retreats to the kitchen where I hear pots and pans clattering.

"You think I want her to be in the middle of this?" I hiss through clenched teeth. "Fuck's sake, Vincenzo."

"I can respect that you're trying to protect her," he says in a lower tone. "It's something Gordo would never have done. But you are smack dab in the center. The only question left is whether you survive it." He leans forward slightly and carefully moves my tea mug from the edge of the table.

I hate how right he is and how deeply it cuts that I can't deny it. "So, what, I cover it up? Lie? Pretend a man didn't get tortured and dumped?" My voice rises and cracks. "Pretend my father isn't a murdering thief and a traitor?" I stutter-breathe at the open confession, though I doubt Rosa heard me. Everyone knows what my father is like, but I've never been put on trial to defend him and I've never had a situation where my life depended on whether I told the truth regarding his crimes.

He doesn't flinch. "You tell them what keeps you breathing. That's the job now." His words are ice cold and wrap around me, chilling me to my core. "It's *your* life that's in your hands, not his."

"You're asking me to betray everything I've worked for." I stand and take a step back, suddenly aware of the space—or lack of it—between us as he rises and stalks toward me.

"I'm telling you that your principles don't mean much if you're in a body bag." His voice is so quiet now, it scares me. The silence after that is thick. He doesn't back down, and I don't have a good enough argument to chase him out now. Besides, who will give me a safe ride home? Those idiots could be waiting for me anywhere.

From the kitchen, Rosa calls, "Either kiss or kill each other. Just leave before more of his type come looking," Rosa calls from the kitchen, completely unfazed.

My cheeks burn.

Vincenzo's eyes stay locked on mine. "We're not done," he growls softly, then he takes me by the elbow as I roll my eyes.

"No," I say. "We never are." I let him drag me toward the door, but I feel scared shitless now.

And God help me, I don't even know what I'll do when I show up to that summons and the *polizia* start asking me questions.

12

VINCENZO

Alessia doesn't argue when I take her by the elbow and walk her to my car. There's a tightness in her jaw, a sluggishness in the way she moves. And her eyes still dart around in fear, which tells me she was really terrified by what happened. I have to look into Leo and where he's at. My gut tells me he's curled up in an alley somewhere bleeding out or already dead. Those fuckers don't mess around.

We drive mostly without words. Rome passes by in streaks of gold and shadow. There isn't much traffic due to the time of the evening, but it's busy enough to give me pauses to glance over at her more than I should. She doesn't look out the window or fidget. Her posture stays rigid, unmoving. She clutches the coat around her like armor, holding it closed as if it can shield her from everything.

"I thought they were going to grab me," she says eventually with a hollow tone. Her eyes stay fixed on the dashboard, but I watch her bottom lip quiver. "I've never been that scared before. Not even when I saw the window broken." Her fingers curl tighter around the belt of her coat.

Comforting someone isn't my strongest quality. I'd like to think I could manage it, but I remain quiet and listen instead. I've been trained to react through violence as a means of self-preservation and defense. Softer things aren't my style.

"It hasn't left me yet," she adds. "That feeling. Like they're still waiting." She exhales slowly, like she's trying to bleed the tension from her chest.

I shift my grip on the wheel and keep my eyes on the road. That, I understand. The feeling of always looking over your shoulder because someone is hunting you. We have that in common.

When we get to her building, I kill the engine and get out. When I open her door, she starts to argue, but I shut it down with a glare. "I'm going in and checking things." I step past her without waiting for permission, and she follows me toward the building. My proximity sensor beeps and I hear her hurried steps as she tries to catch up and keep up.

She unlocks the door and lets us in. The apartment smells like her botanical shampoo. I walk through each room, silently check the closet doors, the windows, the bathroom, and under the bed. I find nothing. The threat must've been only external tonight, but it doesn't make me feel any better about it. If Leo just flaked, I'm gonna tear his throat out.

"Happy?" she says when I return. She stands with her arms crossed, chin lifted like she's trying to prove something.

"You called me because you felt scared," I remind her. "If I'm overstepping, say so. But don't act like I wasn't needed." I meet her eyes, daring her to challenge the truth of it.

"You're not a bodyguard, Vincenzo. You don't have to—" She cuts herself off, frustration tightening her jaw.

"You didn't call a bodyguard. You called me." I don't raise my voice, but my tone stops her cold.

It shuts her up long enough for me to start heading for the door. But when my hand rests on the knob, I hear her whimper and I look over my shoulder.

"Don't go," she says suddenly. "I don't want to be alone." Her voice is quieter now, the edges softened with something raw. Her frustration with me bleeds into desperation to be in control, and while she cannot control me—and she fucking knows it—she has me wrapped around her finger.

I stop and turn fully around, smirking. "Why?"

She steps closer, arms still wrapped tightly around herself. "I feel safer when you're here." She looks at me then, and for once, she doesn't try to hide the desire. Maybe it's just to have my strength so she can sleep knowing I'll kill whoever tries to get at her, or maybe she wants me for me—because there is an electricity that crackles between us.

And it's not the words that hit me. It's the honesty in them. The way her voice doesn't crack, but it wants to. The way her shoulders are still stiff with words she's not ready to say to me yet.

I hold her gaze for a long moment, reading her face the way I would a threat—carefully, thoroughly. Then I take off my coat, hang it on the back of a chair, and walk back into the apartment.

Turning to face her, I see the uncertainty in her eyes, a mixture of gratitude and something else that I can't quite name. I push the thought aside and focus on what's important. Keeping her safe.

"I'll check the locks one more time," I say gruffly, doing my best to maintain a barrier between us. But as I inspect each window and door, I'm acutely aware of her presence behind me, like an electrical current between us. This isn't like me. I never let a mark get under my skin. But Alessia is different.

When I've finished securing the place, I join her in the living room. She's perched on the edge of the couch, her hands clasped tightly in her lap. Her coat is still draped around her shoulders, and she shivers, though I don't know if it's from the chill in the air or something else entirely. "Why don't you change into something more comfortable?" I suggest, trying to divert her attention from her earlier admission. "I'll make us some coffee."

Alessia hesitates, then nods sharply and disappears into her room. I take this opportunity to check the door one last time, making sure it's locked before drawing the blinds. I don't trust whoever it was that harassed her earlier tonight, and I'm determined to keep her safe.

But before I get to the kitchen, I hear movement behind me and she's wearing a soft red robe, cinched at the waist with a matching belt. She pads into the kitchen barefoot and sighs. "I don't think I should have coffee. I won't sleep." Her movements seem robotic, but I give her space.

"Then wine?" I ask, and she nods, moving toward a cupboard on the far end of the kitchen. The curve of her ass is accentuated by the way the robe hugs her hips, and my eyes drink her in. When she stretches up to reach an overhead cupboard but can't quite make it, I walk over and reach it for her. Our bodies are so close I can smell her shampoo, and she doesn't pull away.

"Thanks," she mumbles as I pull two wine glasses out and set them on the counter. She reaches for one as my fingers brush over hers, and the electric charge between us is palpable. I remember the feeling of pinning her to her mattress and I crave more of it. So I don't back away, not even when she pauses and turns, looking up at me. "What?" she breathes, but her heart is pounding. I watch her pulse in her neck throb.

"You're really fucking beautiful, Alessia."

Her cheeks flush crimson, and I reach up and tuck a strand of hair behind her shoulder. "Enzo, I—"

"Shh," I whisper, pressing a finger to her lips. "I'm not going to hurt you, and you don't have to do anything you don't want to. I was just paying you a compliment."

Alessia's lips grow dark with arousal as she reaches up and wraps her fingers around my wrist and pushes my hand down. "Who said I don't want to?"

I let out a loud exhale, unable to control my surprise. "Alessia, I..." I don't know what else to say, because when she looks at me like that, with hunger and vulnerability in her eyes, I'm at a loss for words. Maybe it's the adrenaline from the night's events or the tension that has been building between us since we met, but whatever it is, desire courses through my veins like fire. I shouldn't let my guard down for her. It'll weaken my resolve and my ability to protect her. But here I am, letting her fuck with my head again.

She swallows hard as her eyes flick down to my lips then back to my eyes. "Enzo," she whispers, then steps closer, closing the distance between us. Her lips are soft and tentative as they brush against mine, seeking reassurance. I can't deny her anything in this moment, not when she feels like home in my arms.

My hands curl around her hips, pulling her flush against my body as I feel myself swelling.

I let out a growl of anticipation as I deepen the kiss, savoring the way she tastes, like warmth and sunshine and everything good in this world. Her breath hitches as my tongue slides into her mouth, exploring her sweetness. The soft whimpers that escape her mouth only fan the flames of my desire.

Alessia's hands find their way into my hair, fingers knotting in the dark strands as she pulls me closer. I all but growl against her lips at the invitation, my hand gliding up her robe to cup her ass outside her panties. She moans into my mouth, and I groan in return, desperate to touch more of her fuckable body.

I lift her up, feeling her thighs wrap around my waist as if she were made for me. Her elbows dig into my shoulders as I turn her and slide her ass onto the counter. The wine bottle slides back, but the glasses topple, one of them rolling into the sink where it lands loudly. She doesn't break her concentration on my mouth and deepens her worship of me.

Alessia's lips leave mine to pepper kisses down my jawline, her teeth grazing my skin in the process. The sensation pushes my arousal higher, and I grit my teeth to maintain some semblance of control. But with each flick of her tongue and every nip she leaves behind, my resolve crumbles further. "Fuck, you drive me insane," I growl, grabbing a handful of her hip. Her answer is nothing more than a low moan as she continues her sensual assault on my neck.

My cock strains against my pants, aching for her. I reach between her legs, slipping my hand inside her panties, and she's hot, wet, and ready for me. A groan rumbles through my chest as I tease her entrance before sliding two fingers inside her slowly. She arches into my touch, her nails digging into my shoulders as a whimper escapes her lips.

"Alessia... fuck, I want you so fucking bad."

Her lids are heavy-lidded, a haze of desire clouding them as she struggles to catch her breath. "Christ..." she pants, but I lean in, silencing her with a rough kiss. One hand wanders her body, finding every curve and dip, memorizing them, while the other reaches for my belt. Her hands find mine there and do the work for me by undoing my belt and unzipping my fly.

She guides my hard length through the fly of my pants, and her eyes widen with a mix of awe and lust as she looks down.

"Alessia...look what you do to me," I growl against her ear before sucking her lobe into my mouth. Her answer is to pump her hips against my hand, driving herself deeper onto my fingers as she rocks on the counter's edge.

"You're a little cum slut, aren't you? Just can't get enough of me?" I bite her earlobe, and she hisses.

Alessia's cheeks flame at my crude words, but she doesn't deny it. Instead, she leans in closer, her hot breath on my neck as she nips at my earlobe. "I want you so bad," she moans, her accent thick with need. My self-control, already tenuous, shatters.

I tear the front of her robe open to reveal her perfect tits with pearled nipples. Her hands greedily undo the buttons of my shirt, parting the material as I grip one of her breasts and squeeze. She slides a hand down over my skin, tracing the lines of my tattoos and narrowing her eyes at the dark ink, but I snatch her hand and kiss her palm, then guide her to my cock, where she grips me and begins stroking softly.

"Do you fuck every woman you protect?" she murmurs while I suck her nipples one at a time and keep the pebbled nubs hard and ripe for enjoyment. One of my hands slides back into her panties, hooking a finger through the crotch and pulling hard enough to split the seam. She hisses, and I watch her hips rock again.

"Only the mouthy bitches who beg for it," I growl as I pull her closer to the edge of the counter.

"Do I look like the begging type?" Alessia shudders as I push her hand away from my cock and line it up to her sopping entrance.

"Baby, I can make you beg if you want me to…" My hips push forward, sliding my dick through her slick folds and deep into her core. She groans as I run my hand up her back and tighten my fingers in a fist, knotting her hair around my hand while I begin pumping.

"Make me beg," she grunts. Her neck is arched back so far, she can barely speak. I bite her pulse point hard, and she hisses.

"You asked for it," I growl, my grip tightening in her hair as I plunge into her depths even deeper.

She gasps, every exhale a rib-clenching moan that heightens my arousal. I run my hand down her spine before cupping her ass and slamming us together harder. Her core squeezes me, the tightness driving me insane with lust. "Oh, fuck, Enzo..." she pants, her hips bucking against mine. An animalistic growl escapes my lips as she contradicts herself, one moment telling me to stop, the next urging me on with her body language.

I bite her bottom lip roughly, stealing a messy kiss while my hips piston in and out of hers relentlessly. "Beg me to make you come."

"Please," she whimpers. Her hands are splayed on my chest, fingertips brushing lightly but not making contact with her palms.

"I said beg, dammit," I growl, and her eyes pop open again. They dart around my face and her lip quivers. Alessia's chest heaves, her breaths ragged as she whimpers under my dominant touch. I angle her hips just right, hitting that sweet spot inside her that makes her gasp, then cry out.

"Fuck me," she grunts out between gasps. "Fuck me harder, Enzo." I smirk, my ego stroked by her words. My grip on her hips tightens as I do as she asks.

"Do what to you?" I prod as I bite her chin, then her jaw, then her neck. My cock twitches inside her, the tightening of her slick folds around my shaft almost enough to send me over the edge. I've never wanted something or someone so much in my life, but I hold back. I want to savor this, draw it out and make sure she won't ever forget this night or me.

"Make me come... Please... Oh, God, I'm so close."

"Oh, you like that?" I growl against her ear as I angle my hips upward, hitting that sweet spot again and again. Her moans only intensify, and with each squeeze of her wet center around my cock, my control slips further and further away.

"Say it again," I rasp in her ear, my thrusts unrelenting. "Say you want me to make you come, and it's yours."

"Yes," she moans through gritted teeth, her nails digging into my back. "I want you to make me come, Enzo. Please!"

"That's better." I chuckle darkly before slamming into her one last time, hitting that magic spot so deep inside her that I can feel her orgasm ripple through her body. Her pussy clenches around my dick as her hips rise off the countertop and she screams in pleasure. The sensation sends me over the edge too, and with a low growl, I empty myself into her, my entire body shaking with pleasure.

She shakes and convulses, milking me, and I groan and let the fullness of my release drain every ounce of tension from my body. We're panting, chests heaving from effort, and she clings to me, kissing my chest softly.

Her lips find mine in a sensual exploration as I pull out and let my cum drain from her body. She whimpers when I pull away, but I help her off the counter and make sure she's steady on her feet—weak in the knees—before I finally pull away for good.

Afterward, she opens the bottle and pours herself a drink, then slips her robe back on as she offers me one. Her hands don't shake, but there's tension in the way she holds the glass, like the adrenaline hasn't quite left her system.

"No, thank you... I still have some work to get done tonight." I pick up my clothing, but my mind is already going toward what I have to do next. She's safe here, and I need to post a man at her door now and follow up on why Leo let this shit happen.

I dress quickly, rolling up my sleeves and checking my phone as I slide it back into my jacket pocket. She doesn't try to stop me this time, and I don't explain why I can't stay. There's nothing tender about the silence—only understanding, though I see the hesitancy in her expression.

"What if they come back?"

"They're not coming back tonight. I'll send Rory up and he'll keep watch. You have your weapon... Use it no matter who walks through. My men won't come in unless you ask them." With my clothing back in place, I press a kiss to her forehead and linger for a second. "You're safe, Bella." She's gotten under my skin. She's not just a mark now or someone I protect. She's mine, and every part of my being knows it.

I kiss her one last time and sneak out before she can give me those sad eyes. By the time I make it back to the compound, the gate's locked and the courtyard's quiet. The dogs don't even bark. No one is on the perimeter. I walk up the front steps, already on alert, and that's when I see a flat envelope. The envelope has no label, no return address, and no identifying marks.

My name is printed cleanly in block letters across the front, centered like it was done with care. It hasn't been tossed or slid under the door —it's been placed there intentionally. Meant to be found by me and no one else.

Glancing around to see if I can see the person who left it, I pick it up and take it upstairs, locking the door behind me before I open it. Inside is a flash drive. It's the kind you find at a kiosk or convenience store, plain and cheap—meant to be used once and discarded. Clearly disposable, clearly meant for this moment only. I boot up the laptop I don't keep connected to any network and plug it in.

The file opens without my prompting it, and I stare at the first frame as it comes into focus. It's video footage. Alessia appears on screen.

She's in the lab, running bloodwork, loading samples, scribbling something on a clipboard. The angle is wide, like it was taken from the mounted surveillance unit that's standard there. Which means someone has hacked into the government servers. Someone else is watching her—closely, carefully, and without her knowing.

This isn't just surveillance. It's a message—to me, not her, which means they want me to know they're on to my part in this game we're playing.

I watch until the footage loops, then remove the drive and set it on the desk. I don't crush it because I want to know who sent it, how they got access, and how long they've been this close to her without my knowing.

She called me tonight because she was scared. She asked me to stay because I make her feel safe. But what she doesn't understand is I'm not God and I can't stop the storm that's coming. The Bianchis know what is happening now, and they're not going to quit until they're certain they are secure.

This isn't just a warning.

It's a threat.

13

ALESSIA

I wake alone. The room is quiet except for the faint tick of the wall clock and the hum of morning traffic outside. Soft, golden light filters through the curtains. I lie still, staring at the ceiling, wishing Enzo were here. I'm not scared, but waking to someone in bed with me sounds pleasant and appealing. I've been alone for so long. Maybe I've just lowered my standards too far...

My thoughts drift to yesterday, to the footsteps behind me. The way my skin prickled. I tried really hard to convince myself it was nothing, but when Enzo left his friend Rory outside my door, I couldn't ignore it anymore. Even Enzo thinks there is an additional threat, and that turns my stomach.

I push myself out of bed and force myself to shower and get ready, but by the time I get to work, my nerves are stretched thin. The lab's usual chill does nothing to ground me the way a temperature drop can do to the nervous system. I log in, sterilize my instruments, and begin the routine. It's easier when my hands are moving—when the science takes over.

There's a new body on the slab, a teenager—car accident victim—so I dig into what seems normal. But routine shatters fast when Dr. Bernardi corners me over the exam table, waving a folder like it's a death sentence.

"The 416-bis investigators pulled your toxicology report," he says. His voice is too loud, too self-satisfied. "They flagged it as incomplete. Why isn't it finished?"

He tosses the printout onto the counter and my stomach flips. It's the preliminary report I ran on Matteo Vescari's blood panel, and I know it's clean. I didn't destroy evidence. I just didn't submit everything yet because I'm not sure what to do. I know what the right thing to do is, but Enzo makes it so difficult to know the right thing for my family.

"What do you want me to say?" I ask, refocusing on the exposed chest cavity of this victim. Her parents want to know exactly what caused the death, as if saying "traumatic physical injury due to blunt-force trauma at a high rate of speed" isn't enough.

"Say you're going to get ahead of it," Luca replies. "Because right now, it looks like you're either sloppy or dragging your feet. Why isn't this finished?"

I wait until he walks off—the smug bastard—before I exhale.

There's no point in trying to deny that I'm procrastinating, but since my boss is leaning on me harder than normal for this one, I do have to do something. I can't just publish my findings. I'm not as much worried whether my father goes to prison as I am concerned about what Enzo may think of me. And if he's right and it starts some sort of meltdown of the criminal organizations in the city, wouldn't that be a good thing?

But then who would let my name slip? Because the Costa legacy is so far-reaching that for sure, someone would tie me to it. I've done nothing wrong, but simply by association, they would label me as dangerous. And given that I've hidden some things in this Vescari case already, I may face penalties anyway. I feel stuck.

That night, I stay late, long after the hallway lights have dimmed and the cleaning staff have moved on. I seal myself in my office and lay out the original blood samples, double-checking each slide as if I might've missed something the first time. The data is clean and my work is good, but the implications are murky. If I submit the full report as is, it could unravel the carefully curated narrative the Bianchis are pushing—the one Enzo wants buried (A.K.A. the truth). If I delay, I risk being flagged for obstruction.

Either way, someone will come for me.

I open a fresh analysis window on my terminal and begin drafting a revised report. I don't fabricate evidence—but I do add enough ambiguity to justify a longer timeline because I have to think this through. I adjust the toxin markers, cite additional metabolite discrepancies, and insert a paragraph explaining the need for further confirmatory tests.

Each keystroke feels like a betrayal. I'm not sure if it's to the truth, to my profession, or to myself. But I do it anyway. I have to. Buying time is the only strategy left that doesn't end in immediate fallout.

When I finally hit *Save*, the digital timestamp glares back at me. My hands are trembling. I lock the file, encrypt it, and sit back in my chair, heart pounding in my throat.

Vincenzo's words echo in my head. "You play both sides long enough, and someone will make you choose."

When exhaustion threatens to keep me holed up in the lab, I gather my things and leave the lab, walk the shadowed streets home, lock the door behind me, and turn off every light but the one in the kitchen. I sit on the edge of the sofa for a while, still in my work clothes, trying to convince myself that what I did tonight was necessary, but the guilt is cloying, swarming me like angry birds in that Hitchcock film.

When the buzzer sounds, I already know who it is. I don't question the timing or ask why he's here. I rise slowly, cross the quiet apartment, and undo the chains and deadbolts.

I open the door and Vincenzo stands there in a dark coat, eyes scanning my face. One eyebrow is raised as he leans on the jamb and says, "Shift change. I gave Rory the night off. I'll be sitting here if you need me." It's kind of him to let me know. I appreciate it, but I feel reserved.

Maybe he thinks I'm breaking. Maybe he's here to catch me in the middle of something damning. But when I meet his gaze, it doesn't feel like surveillance. It feels like a moment where he's waiting to be invited in, like because I've let my guard down around him, I'll want him inside, when I would let his men just park their asses in the hallway.

He's not wrong.

I step back to let him in. "Couch is yours," I say as I close the door behind him, and this time, I mean the couch, though I wouldn't mind being held, but things are already messy and complicated. If I end up swinging toward Dr. Bernardi and letting the case go to the investigators, I'd like a bit of cushion for my heart because Enzo won't be happy with me.

He nods once, shrugs off his coat, and drops it on the back of a kitchen chair. He doesn't press me with questions or remind me how I'm supposed to be hiding evidence and throwing a case. I appreciate that more than I want to admit.

I go to my room without another word, peel off my work clothes, and slip under the covers. But I can't sleep. My body is still humming from the choice I made tonight. I stare at the ceiling again, aware of every creak and shift in the silence of my apartment for more than an hour.

And I know… I didn't leave the door open by mistake.

14

VINCENZO

I sit up slowly, rubbing a hand over my face. The apartment is dim, the haze of middle-night graying the windows. For a second, I think I imagined the crying. Then I hear it again—a broken breath, a tremor in the dark.

I stand without making a sound. The couch creaks under my weight, but nothing else stirs. Her bedroom door is cracked an inch, the light inside faint. I move toward it with slow, controlled steps, then I push it open with two fingers.

Alessia is curled into herself on the far side of the bed, knees drawn up, one arm shielding her face. The other is clenched in the sheets and her shoulders are shaking.

For a second, my mind runs through the worst-case scenarios. If someone hurt her, if someone got past me, I'll never forgive myself. And Gordo? Gordo will make sure I never draw another breath. He may not have sent me here at all, but men are fiercely protective of their daughters and wives.

But there's no blood. No signs of a break-in. Just Alessia, breaking apart under her covers over something that's tormenting her in her mind. I stand there watching for a moment, listening to her soft sobs and stuttered breaths, unaware that her eyes are open and she can see me.

She turns her head slightly when I shift my weight to lean on the door frame. "I'm fine," she says, voice raw and tight. She doesn't lift her head or chase me away, but she pulls the blanket higher like it might shield her from my presence. "You don't have to—"

"Don't lie," I say softly. My hand lingers on the doorframe, but I take a step into her room to close the distance between us. When she was terrified last week, I was the one she called for comfort, and tonight she cries alone. That fact doesn't escape me. But then, I'm not the sort of guy who offers a shoulder to cry on very often.

When I walk toward the bed, she doesn't argue, doesn't sit up or try to pull herself together to dissuade me. She lies there limp with her strength drained, and I perch on the edge of the mattress, knowing that I won't get back to sleep again tonight.

Several seconds pass in the silence, and then she lifts one hand toward me, palm open in the space between us. It's not just a gesture, it's an answer to the question I didn't ask. I move before I think. I take off my jeans and slide in behind her. I don't ask questions or press her to explain.

Curling around her, I breathe her in, and when her fingers find mine, I let her pull me closer. The mattress dips beneath my weight, and for a moment neither of us says anything. Her back is to me, but I feel every tremor that moves through her frame. She doesn't resist. If anything, she presses closer.

I feel her breaths slow against my chest. Her hand finds the fabric of my T-shirt and grips it. There's nothing I can say to fix whatever woke her, though I have a good idea of what it is. She's in an impossible situation, being asked to take a side in a war that's not her own. I can't blame her for wrestling with it, and if it were up to me, I would destroy the entire world to set her free.

But all I can do is hold her.

The minutes stretch, long and quiet. I lie still, focused on the steady rhythm of her breathing, the warmth of her body against mine. Outside, the city begins to wake. The early drone of traffic builds beneath the apartment window. Her trembling slows gradually until the tension leaves her shoulders and she lies still in my arms.

When she finally speaks, her voice is soft enough I almost miss it. "I don't think I can handle this." She turns her chin upward so our eyes meet.

I tighten my hold. "You don't have to do it alone." I press my palm flat against her back, feeling the shallow rise and fall of each breath.

She exhales slowly, then whispers, "Bernardi cornered me again. He said the 416-bis investigation is reviewing my toxicology work. I panicked. I didn't lie, exactly, but I manipulated the results. Stalled for time." Her words tremble as much as her body did earlier.

I brush my thumb along her spine. "I can't buy you time, Alessia. All I can do is promise to back you up if you do what's right—for your family, and for yourself."

She shifts in the silence that follows, then turns fully into me and kisses me softly. At first I think of pushing her away, of shaking her and reminding her how dangerous this is. I may be watching her, following her around town, but I can't be with her every second of the day. And what happened to Leo—how I found him gutted behind the lab in a puddle of his own blood, urine, and feces—it could happen to her.

But I kiss her back with equal pressure instead, because I'll never coerce her into anything. Gordo tried that and she ran from him. I won't do that to her. But I will do my damnedest to try to show her the light.

Our bodies fit together effortlessly as if they were meant to be intertwined like this. I deepen the kiss, my hands gripping her hips to bring her closer as our tongues dance in heated strokes. Her hands roam up my back, entangling in my hair, her nails raking against my scalp in a delicious torture.

With a muffled moan, she grinds against my thigh, and I feel myself starting to swell. Her scent inflames my senses further, clouding any remaining sense of self-preservation or restraint I have. Starting my day with a good fuck has never been so tempting, and I don't even fight the sense that I should be getting up and heading out. I pull her on top of me and grip her panties, sliding them down over her hips.

Alessia's breath hitches as I bare her silky thighs and part her folds, exposing her slick entrance to the cold air. Her readiness for me emboldens my desire. I drag her hips closer, rubbing my hard length against her heat, teasing us both with the anticipation of what's to come.

"Why do you want me so bad?" I grumble as she tugs at my shirt, trying to rid me of it. She gasps and snickers as I sit up and tear it off, nearly tossing her from my lap.

"Why do you keep coming back? Can't you stay away?" she purrs, sliding her fingers into the hem of my boxers.

"Why would I want to deprive myself of this?" My lips close on hers again as I work the hem of her nightgown upward. They break contact momentarily as I pull it over her head, and then I push her shoulders as I lie down, so the light from the city outside her window illuminates her bare skin as she straddles me.

"Make me your fuck toy, Enzo," Alessia moans, and I have no problem doing that. I hook my thumbs in my boxers and lift my hips to shove them down, and she grunts and shifts as I peel the last remaining fabric away that separates our bodies.

It drifts to the floor, and our eyes lock in the dim light of her room. Hers are hooded with desire and a touch of defiance, as if she's daring me to do my worst. My cock twitches in anticipation, aching to be inside her again.

I tighten my grip on her hips, hoisting her higher as she positions me at her entrance. Slowly, oh, so slowly, I press inside her willing heat, savoring the exquisite sensation of her tightness clenching around me. Her fingers wrap around slats in the headboard above our heads as she releases a guttural moan, her hips arching back against me as she takes it all in.

She's insatiable, hungry for more of what I can give her. And I'm all too willing to oblige. She starts grinding, tits swaying as she rocks her head back and lets her hair dangle down her back. I grip her tits hard, pearling the nipples between my fingertips. She hisses and groans as she takes control, and I let her think she's in charge as I press a thumb to her clit and swirl it in her moisture.

Alessia's breath hitches as I pull her hair, my fingers tangling in the dark locks as she rocks back and forth, impaling herself on my cock in a relentless rhythm. Sweat glistens on our skin, the room heavy with the scents of sex and submission. This soft, willing act is a far cry from the feisty woman Gordo hired me to protect, but I'm not one to deny a good thing.

Her walls clench around me, squeezing me, milking me for every drop of pleasure I can give her. "Harder," she pants, so I do as she commands, driving into her deeper and faster, our bodies slapping together with the same desperate intensity as before. Her nails rake up and down my chest, leaving stinging welts in their wake, and when I can't take it anymore, I flip her over hard, tossing her down on the mattress.

She gasps and her eyes go wide momentarily before I flip her again so her ass is in the air and her face is buried in the pillows. I grip my cock, stroking a few times as I line up to her other hole and press there.

"I need this," I tell her as I start pushing hard, and she grunts and spits as I thrust in.

Alessia's moans intensify, muffled by the pillow beneath her as I push further. Her body tenses around me, walls clenching and unclenching around my thick girth. Slowly, I ease in and out, working past her tight ring of muscles until she begins to relax. Her moans become higher pitched and desperate, her hips rocking to meet my rhythm as I piston in and out of her firm ass. Her hands bunch the comforter in fists at her sides, knuckles white against the black fabric.

"Oh, fuck," she gasps. "Fuck me, Enzo." As if I need any further invitation. I press on harder and faster, smacking her ass and leaving bright red handprints beneath my fingers. She moans and bucks against me, begging for more. She reaches between her thighs and rubs herself, desperately trying to get release, and I pull her hair a bit harder as I pound.

"That's right... You like it rough, don't you? Beg for your reward."

Tremblingly, she cries out, "Yes, fuck me harder! I–I love it! Please... need you so much!" In response, I pull back and plunge deeper into her, eliciting a long moan from the both of us. My balls contract. I grunt out her name as wave after wave of cum blasts into her hungry ass, her tight ring of muscles squeezing every drop out of me in a delicious, drawn-out orgasm.

Alessia shakes and jolts. It takes both hands on her hips to hold her up while trying to balance, and she convulses and shakes the bed. Her body begins to slow down and she goes limp.

When I pull out, she slumps to the side, and I flop to the bed next to her and pull her back into my chest to hold her. Her breathing is so heavy I can feel her entire body pulse with each heartbeat. Her eyes shut. I press a kiss to her temple and peel a curl of hair off her cheek that clings with sweat.

"Thank you," she breathes, and I pull her tighter. We lie in each other's arms for a long while as the sun continues rising and the room grows brighter.

She falls asleep quickly, her breaths evening out as she rests against me. Her hand stays tangled in the fabric of the sheets, and I don't move for a long time. The light outside shifts slowly, revealing daybreak, but inside it's still and warm.

I study the shape of her mouth, the delicate rise of her cheek, and the tension that's finally drained from her body. For a while, I let myself believe she's safe here. That whatever storm waits for us can't reach her in this moment. But one wrong choice, one wrong move and everything will crumble around her. It's why I have to go.

Before the sun fully rises, I slip out of bed, gather my clothes, dress in silence, and leave the apartment without waking her. By the time I reach the abandoned shipping yard, where the trail from the SIM card has led me to a rusted chain-link gate outside Luca Bernardi's old research lab, it's almost midday. Before he was hired by the Ministry of Justice. The building is supposed to be shuttered, but a dim light flickers inside.

I push open the door very slowly and step into a mostly gutted workspace. Dust clings to every surface. Cabinets stand half-open and the air is stale with disuse. In the far corner, Luca is bent over a box of papers, stuffing files into a leather satchel. When I discovered the information in the SIM led here, I wondered why. But it makes sense if Vescari was trying to send a message to him. One that I will never deliver.

He looks up when he hears me. His face remains expressionless for a moment before he scowls. He doesn't flinch or recoil, and he doesn't bother to feign surprise. He simply straightens slowly, like he's been expecting interference, and lets his hand rest deliberately on top of the box in front of him.

"Cleaning house?" I ask, keeping my tone even.

He zips the satchel closed with an exaggerated slowness. "They're shutting down the lab for good. Thought I'd take my souvenirs."

I carefully circle as I ask him, "What have you been feeding the *polizia*?" I'm not hopeful he will give me any real answers, but curiosity killed the cat.

He laughs—actually laughs. "They don't need me to feed them anything. The 416-bis task force already has enough to burn every syndicate from here to Palermo."

My grip tightens. "If that were true, there would be a manhunt going and I would be in prison instead of here with you." His expression darkens further and he picks up his bag defensively, jerking it toward himself.

Before he can answer, a metallic clatter sounds outside. I step back into a shadowy place by the window, drawing my gun in one smooth motion. I angle toward the door just as it bursts open.

Inspector Elena Greco storms in, two plainclothes officers flanking her. She takes one look at me and pulls her weapon before I can think. I will not fire first and be tried for attacking an officer of the law, but I won't hesitate to defend myself.

Greco looks annoyed, but her men look terrified. They know who I am, by the looks of it, and the weaselly way Bernardi slithers out the door to his own escape only makes this ripe with questions.

"Put it down, Morelli! Now!" Greco points her gun at me but doesn't fire.

One of her men doesn't wait, though. He fires, and the shot cracks past my ear and punches a hole in the wall behind me.

I duck and return fire once—just enough to make them scatter. The man dives to the floor following his buddy beside him, and Greco shouts again, but I'm already moving. I cut through the back hallway, shove through a rusted exit door, and disappear into the yard's maze of shipping containers.

Gunfire explodes behind me as I run, the sound tearing through the warehouse like thunder. The two plainclothes officers shout to each other, their boots pounding after mine. I vault over a tipped cart and duck behind a support column as bullets chew into the walls around me. Concrete dust showers down from the roofing overhead.

I catch my breath for half a second, then move again quickly with focus. I round the corner and hear them split—one looping left, the other trying to flank me. Greco's voice cuts through the chaos, barking orders I don't stop to decipher.

The back gate is rusted, but not locked. I slam it open with my shoulder and spill out of the shipping yard into an alleyway only blocks from my car. Sunlight flashes off the metal containers, disorienting me for just a second, but I keep moving, weaving between parked cars and listening for pursuit.

One of them fires again. The round hits a shipping container with a hollow clang just on the other side of the fence, but they can't get to me without going to the gate first. I don't stop. I dive between two cars, leap a broken pallet, and disappear down a side alley choked with weeds and dumpsters.

By the time they reach the edge of the yard, I'm gone.

Greco probably thought she was going to nail me the second she saw me, and she's likely very pissed that I got away. Her men won't hear the end of it.

But something fruitful came of that. Bernardi is scared stiff. He is boxing up any trace of old casefiles he's worked on because he knows we're not going to take this sitting down. Covering his ass is the only play he has since he doesn't have enough evidence to go full-bore with the investigation without Alessia.

LEONA WHITE

The bad news is now he will lean on her harder, and I'm not sure if she can take it.

15

ALESSIA

The hum of the centrifuge blends with the soft tick of the wall clock, both keeping time in a room where it feels like everything has stopped. I lean over the workstation and label the third vial, double-checking the barcode before slotting it into the rack. The blood samples are from a more recent case—smaller, less politically charged—but my hands still move with care. Repetition is comfort. Procedure is safety.

I key in the parameters for a toxin panel and let the machine begin its cycle. While it runs, I turn to the freezer and retrieve an old sample, not part of any open report. Just something I've been holding off on. I log it unofficially, outside the system, and run a quick protein degradation test—not because it's necessary, but because I want to see how well it's held up.

The screen lights up with the initial results, displaying a clean molecular structure and only minor signs of degradation. The data is strong—consistent, intact, and suitable for full sequencing without requiring another extraction. I document the findings, write a brief note for my records, and file the report manually. Afterward, I back up the file to my encrypted drive, locking it away until I decide what to do next.

It's not what I planned to do today, but it keeps my hands moving. And right now, with everything on my mind, it's what I need it to do. I keep glancing at the profile from under Matteo's fingernails, unable to stop myself. I already know it's a familial match, but not knowing exactly who it belongs to has been eating at me. I keep wondering if it could be Uncle Emilio. If this whole time, I've been assuming one betrayal while missing another, the only way to be sure is to test it against my own blood.

I pull a fresh needle from the sterile tray and secure the tourniquet around my arm. My fingers tremble slightly as I disinfect the skin and slide the needle in. The blood fills the vial in a steady stream. It is bright and warm as it rises to the fill line, clearly and undeniably mine. I remove the tourniquet, press gauze to the puncture, and label the sample, but not with my own name.

I can't use recycled data or archived controls. I need to know for certain, not just clinically, but with everything in me. So, I load the fresh sample into the analyzer and begin configuring the comparison parameters.

This test isn't just a step in the process—it's a decision. I'm running my blood against the unknown profile pulled from under Matteo's nails. I already know what it'll show, but the certainty of seeing it confirmed on the screen forces me to face it. Knowing in theory is one thing. Watching it unfold in real time is something else entirely.

I need the truth to stare back at me so I can't look away. So it will force me to finally make my choice—the one Enzo is pushing for.

The screen flickers, then begins processing. Each pass tightens something in my chest. Watching the confirmation crawl line by line onto the screen feels different.

The final line appears on the screen. *Match Probability 99.9%.* The comparison is statistically conclusive. The sample from beneath Matteo Vescari's fingernails shares a near-identical mitochondrial profile with my own, narrowing the source to a direct paternal relative. That leaves only one possibility. Not a cousin. Not a distant uncle. My father.

The screen doesn't spell out his name, but it doesn't have to. The probability leaves no room for doubt. It hits me like a gut punch and I feel like I will throw up.

My hand falls away from the console. I brace against the edge of the desk, willing myself to breathe through it.

I thought I understood what the data meant. I told myself I was prepared. But now that it's confirmed, the reality feels like a collapse inside my chest. The certainty cuts deeper than suspicion ever could. I stare at the readout and feel everything shift. I don't know how to move forward with this truth lodged so firmly inside me, but I know I can't pretend I never saw it.

The data confirms direct contact at the time of Matteo's death. The DNA wasn't deposited days before or transferred by casual proximity. It was introduced during the critical window, when he was killed, and from a source so genetically close, there's no plausible alternative.

Vescari clawed my father's body somewhere, and his blood got lodged under the dead man's fingernails. It means if I saw my father, there would be no mistaking the scratches, probably on his arms, neck, or face. I shake my head and stare blankly at the screen.

If I submit this, the 416-bis investigation has what it needs to file the charges. This finding ties my father directly to the murder. And if it ties my father, it ties Emilio and Enzo and the whole damn organization. It's a smoking bullet, and I'm the only one who knows about it.

I sit back in my chair feeling lightheaded. My hand hovers over the upload key, then falls to my side.

Instead, I quickly store the results on a local drive. I encrypt the file, store it on a local drive, and isolate it from the main system. It remains invisible unless someone knows exactly where to look. I can't bring myself to destroy the evidence, but I can't very well send it in.

A few seconds later, an email from Dr. Bernardi lights up my inbox. The message is polite on the surface, couched in professionalism, but there's tension beneath every line. It's a reminder to comply with the task force by the end of the week, phrased like a courtesy but meant as pressure.

I stare at the screen for a long moment, then close the program without saving anything more. I push back from the desk, heart racing, and pull out my phone. My hands are unsteady as I scroll to Enzo's contact and hit *Dial*. He picks up before the second ring.

"Alessia? Is everything okay?" His voice is instantly comforting, but I'm not foolish enough to say much over the phone.

"Uh, I'm ready to go home. I'd like it if you could come to the back door..." My voice cracks as I speak, and at the same time, I stand and collect my purse and coat. He can't park on the property, but the back door of the lab opens to an alley where he can meet me in a few strides instead of the thirty-meter block.

"Yeah, of course. You sound rattled."

"Enzo... It was him." I can't say much more than that, but based on how he hangs up the phone, I know he understands that I won't.

My eyes flick around nervously as I keep a lookout for Dr. Bernardi on my way toward the back. I don't need another lecture about being prompt with my report, and if he came at me now, I would probably crack open like a peanut shell.

Enzo is already waiting at the curb, engine idling, as I slip out the rear exit and cross the short stretch of pavement. I open the passenger door and climb in without a word. He puts the car in gear and pulls away from the curb like we're just leaving for dinner, not spiriting away from a lie I've been thinking of telling.

For a few blocks, I don't speak. I keep my eyes on the windshield, hands clenched in my lap. Finally, I say, "The mitochondrial match came back at 99.9 percent. It's my father."

Enzo keeps one hand on the wheel as he reaches to rest the other on my knee. It's a bold move since we're not truly a couple, but I don't mind. It comforts me. "Have you made up your mind?" he asks, flicking glances at me.

"I'm freaking out. I want to do the right thing." I cover my face to hide my shame, but there's no hiding from him.

He glances at me again, then back at the road, and his grip on my knee tightens. "Right for who?"

"I don't know. I can't think straight." I'm shaking my head, willing this entire situation to go away so I can go back to being normal again.

His voice is quiet, but firm. "If the Costas go down, they'll drag you with them. You're not far enough removed. And if they fall, the Bianchis won't be far behind. I'll be in prison. I won't be able to protect you from any of them."

I stare out the window, the city lights smearing across the glass as we pass them. My throat tightens, but I force myself to breathe slowly, to keep from unraveling in front of him. I can't answer him yet. Every possible outcome feels like a trap. Every choice leads to someone bleeding, maybe even dying. And all of it circles back to me.

I press my fingers to my temples, willing the world to slow down.

16

VINCENZO

Emilio doesn't flinch when I say the words. He leans back in his chair without hesitation and exhales a long string of cigar smoke like he expected this all along.

"So it's Gordo." He leans forward slightly, folding his hands, cigar pinched between two fingers. His slightly balding head shines with sweat and he stares at me in anger.

"It's a ninety-nine point nine percent match. Blood from under Matteo's fingernails. Alessia reran it herself against her own blood." I watch his expression for a flicker of surprise, but there's none.

He taps his knuckles on the table once and sits back, scrubbing his face with a hand. "Goddammit, Gordo, what were you thinking?"

"It's enough to file charges. Enough to trigger the rest of the case." I know what he will say. He's going to tell me to off Bernardi, but it won't make a difference at this point. I don't think it ever would've. The push for the investigation came from higher up all along.

His gaze sharpens. "And she hasn't turned it in?" The way his eyes narrow in skepticism doesn't surprise me, either. He thinks Alessia is just going to roll on him because she cut ties, but he can't see that even to her, blood means something. Or maybe my warning about other crime families coming after her is what's holding her back.

"Not yet. She's rattled, but I think she's shaking in the right direction." I keep my tone even, though I can already feel where this conversation is heading.

Emilio nods slowly, then sits forward again. "Then it's time to tighten our hold. You keep her contained. And I want Luca Bernardi under pressure. Maybe we can squeeze him so he'll back off now." He pushes back from the table and levels his gaze at me like he's already handed down an order I can't question.

I want to protest this move, but I know when to question him and when to leave it alone. So I get up and walk out with plans to go find Bernardi and lean on him a little. I'm not foolish enough to think it will work, but I can try.

The minute I'm in the car, I start making calls. I know Luca. He's slippery, the kind of man who never parks in the same place twice unless he feels protected. It takes a few hours, but I trace him to a secure hotel on the edge of Trastevere. The place is discreet, shielded from outside view, and fully outfitted with deep surveillance wiring throughout the property that they call a security system, but I know how to avoid the cameras.

I park two blocks away and kill the engine and the lights. The hotel is tall and tucked into a narrow street, its entrance partially obscured by a row of hedges and a discreet security kiosk. Just before ten p.m., movement flickers in the lobby. Luca appears wearing a pressed suit. His posture is relaxed and self-satisfied. The smirk he wears hasn't changed since the day I met him, and every time I see it, I imagine how it would feel to drive my fist into it.

I step out of the car and begin my approach. My plan is to get him to a quiet location where I can lay some heavy threats on his shoulders. If he's running scared, he'll make mistakes, and maybe he will be intimidated enough to turn Greco away.

Except, as I approach the front entrance, I notice movement from the corner of my eye.

Elena Greco enters the lobby from the side corridor, walking with purpose. Her shoulders are squared and her chin held high. She doesn't flash a badge or speak to the desk clerk. She walks directly toward Bernardi who stands and extends a hand to shake hers.

I freeze mid-step and duck behind a pillar, shifting to keep the reflection of the glass entryway in view. Luca greets her near the elevators. They speak without looking around, without checking the exits, and without the kind of stiffness that comes from official oversight. Their body language is calm, coordinated. They're smiling and laughing like old friends, like this a hookup or a date. They know each other well, which means if I push on Bernardi, he won't hesitate to tell Greco.

I narrow my eyes and step back into the shadows, feeling anger clamp down on my chest. The state *polizia* aren't circling. They've already had the full goddamn plan laid out. I'm shocked charges haven't been filed already.

I don't make the mistake of getting closer. I move quickly but carefully, keeping to the edges of the lot until I slip through a side door back into the parking garage. The overhead lights flicker, and my footsteps echo over the concrete. I force myself to breathe evenly even though my pulse is racing in anger.

Once I reach my car, I duck into the driver's seat and pull the door closed without slamming it. The lock clicks into place. I wait until the door locks behind me before pulling out my burner and dialing Emilio. I get straight to the point.

"They've already got to Bernardi," I say as I stare through the windshield, watching shadows crawl across the hotel's concrete face. "An agent, Greco, is meeting him directly right now."

I can hear the pressure building in my chest as I adjust myself in my seat and start the car with the phone pressed tight to my ear. Bernardi thinks Alessia is going to produce, and that means a massive investigation—bigger than what they've already got going. And if he's with Greco in a federal safe zone, it means they're not just building the case—they're close to launching it. Every second I stood outside that hotel, I felt the window closing.

They're about to move.

"We need to shut this down," Emilio snaps. I can hear movement on his end, the rustle of papers or maybe something heavier. "Kill him."

"Boss, it's too late for that. Greco won't care if Bernardi goes missing. All she is waiting on is the report Alessia serves up." My voice drops as I look over my shoulder, making sure I wasn't followed.

It's no longer hearsay. The evidence is solid and admissible. They have evidence if Alessia hands it over. They have solid backing—documentation from the lab, authenticated files, and a verifiable chain of custody that connects every piece of evidence. And they are executing a coordinated strategy, drawing the net tighter with every move.

Emilio swears loudly on the other end, a string of curses so sharp I pull the phone away from my ear. "Handle it, Enzo. I don't care how. Just make it go away," he barks, and then the line goes dead.

I sit in silence, gripping the wheel with both hands as I stare through the windshield. Every thought collides at once—Bernardi digging, Greco closing in, Emilio barking orders like blood can patch holes. I blink hard and exhale slowly, trying to settle the chaos pressing behind my eyes. But the silence doesn't calm me—it sharpens things. The moment has shifted. I shift into gear and pull away from the curb. I don't know what I'll say when I see Alessia, but I know where I need to be.

I pull up near her building to check the perimeter before I head up. It's habit now after what happened to Leo.

A dark sedan sits across the street with its engine off and lights dimmed, parked in a position that offers an unobstructed view of the building's entrance. It doesn't belong to us and I study it from a distance for a moment. But I notice the state polizia plate on the back, and my gut twists. I walk past it slowly, then double back behind a row of scooters and stare at it in anger.

I can't just leave it alone. I cross the street, step up to the driver's side window, and knock hard. The tinted glass doesn't roll down right away, so I knock again, harder this time. When it does lower, the man inside looks at me like he's annoyed. Mid-forties, clean-shaven, trying too hard to look unremarkable.

"You lost?" I ask, keeping my voice even.

He doesn't answer but he shifts his hand toward the console, maybe going for a badge or maybe a weapon, but I don't back down because if they're camping out here, they have a reason. I need to know that reason.

"If you're watching her, you'd better make sure someone's watching you." The hem of my jacket flaps in the breeze and I grab it, holding it open so he can see what I mean. The guy is too old for this job, past his prime, and judging by the fear in his eyes, I'd say he understands who I am.

He mutters something about doing his job, then jerks the car into gear. The tires bark against the pavement as he pulls away so fast he almost runs my toes over.

I race to my car and swing onto the street behind him. He guns it through the intersection and I follow, tires squealing as I take the corner hard. He cuts across two lanes of traffic and dives into a roundabout without signaling, forcing a scooter to veer wide and just miss him. I don't lose ground. My focus narrows.

He accelerates down a wide avenue lined with row houses and throws another sharp left, nearly clipping a garbage bin. I stay on his bumper.

Horns blare behind us as I cut through the same turn, pushing the car harder than I should. He heads toward the edge of the district, where streetlights grow sparse and the pavement's more pothole than road.

I see him glance back through the rearview mirror. He doesn't know the city like I do. He's panicking now, swerving toward a narrow underpass near the train yard. I follow him in and the world closes down—concrete on both sides, flashing lights overhead, the high-pitched whine of my tires echoing.

He breaks out onto an access road and takes a hard right. But there's a truck backing into a loading dock, blocking most of the lane. I veer wide, trying to keep sight of him as he disappears between two shipping containers at the far end of the lot. And my car smashes into two trash bins out for collection night and I'm forced to slam on the brakes to avoid hitting the truck.

By the time I make the turn, he's gone.

I ease off the gas and coast to a stop. He's out of sight, but he won't forget the message. The Costas are still in this game and we're not backing down without a fight.

17

ALESSIA

The hotel bar is all polished wood and Italian leather, with low amber light that casts everything in the same forgiving glow. I nurse a Negroni and try not to look anxious, but the back of my dress is damp where it sticks to the velvet booth, and I cross my legs slowly, careful not to flash too much skin.

Luca Bernardi is already three drinks in when he arrives. He doesn't sit right away. He stands at the edge of the table like he's waiting for an invitation, as if this is some dinner date instead of the power play it is. He demanded that we meet off the record, away from work, said he didn't want certain things overheard on government servers or passed through departmental gossip. I didn't argue, because if he knows something, I need to know what.

"Alessia," he says, voice slurring at the edges. "If you're sitting on anything—evidence, reports, even loose threads—it's time to decide how this ends." His fingers dust over the table's smooth surface as he eyes me menacingly. I'm not coughing up what I know, and he'll never find my evidence, either—not unless I want him to. But for that I'd need assurances.

"You're late," I reply, swirling the ice in my glass. "But I guess that's in character." My nonchalance is totally faked. My heart is a jackhammer against my ribs.

He smirks and slides into the seat across from me as he unbuttons his jacket and smooths his tie across his chest. He has no drink in hand, but a dark, smug smirk is on his face. As if that's supposed to intimidate me. He has no clue I've been fucking the devil. Dr. Bernardi doesn't scare me at all right now.

"They're close to making the case," he says like it's a casual update. "We could be days away." I can smell the stench of whiskey on his breath, which means he was either in the men's room when I got here, having drunk a lot before that point, or he was elsewhere getting sloshed before he arrived.

My throat tightens. "The Vescari case?"

He nods, gesturing for another drink. "Not just him. Gordo Costa's name is coming up more and more." He narrows his eyes at me darkly and his smirk deepens. "And you know what happens once his name's on paper. It pulls everyone in his orbit under the microscope."

I keep my face neutral, but my heart is galloping. The implication hits hard and fast. He doesn't say my name specifically, but he doesn't have to. I hid evidence. I altered timelines. Even if I course-correct now, I'm tainted.

And why did he name my father directly? It could have been a slip or a warning. But if Luca has figured out who I am—if he knows that Gordo Costa isn't just a name in a file but the man who raised me—then it's over. My professional cover, my name, my carefully built life —all of it collapses.

He doesn't know what I know. He hasn't seen the DNA match. But if he starts connecting dots and decides to use my bloodline against me, he won't need a warrant to get what he wants. He'll just lean in and remind me who I belong to.

"The task force is already building their indictment list," he says as the bartender approaches. "It won't just be bosses. It'll be lieutenants, fixers, medical professionals. Anyone who knew and didn't act." His attention turns to the slender, twiggy man with tattoos up and down his arms as he gives a drink order, but my spine stiffens.

I glance at the mirrored wall behind him and see my reflection waver, distorted slightly by the bevel in the glass. My skin looks pale and clammy. My eyes are sunken and dark circles ring them. It could be the lighting, but my guess is it's just the anxiety-sickness taking me over.

He leans in. "You think you'll get immunity if you share now?"

"I haven't made any discoveries," I say carefully, because that's the narrative I've set up. That is what I told them. I needed more time for more testing, but it feels like time is up.

"Sure you haven't." He grins, teeth slightly bared. "That's why you're here, right? Because you like the suspense and the back and forth. Or maybe it's because you know exactly how close we are. Maybe you're trying to decide whether you want to go down with your father or hand us something that lets you walk away."

A sudden chill makes me shiver as I process the implications of what he just said. "You think Gordo Costa is my father?" The words come out hollow because I feel gutted.

He tilts his head. "You changed your name—moved across the country. You expect me to believe you did that for the view?" The bartender brings a glass tumbler with a few fingers of whiskey in it and sets it in front of him, which serves as a slight distraction from the way I'm feeling cornered.

My throat is dry. I stare into my glass as the adrenaline courses through me, making me shake. "That's a serious accusation."

"I've seen enough to know who you are, Alessia, and I have proof." He lets the words hang between us, heavy with implication. I squeeze my clutch to my stomach, scrambling for a justification that might deflect his aim. But there's nothing clean to reach for.

Everything I've done to protect myself—changing my name, transferring cities, building a clean record—suddenly looks like deliberate misdirection. A façade, a cover story laid too neatly. In this context, it makes me look like I was planted where I am just to cover for my father's illegal activities.

He leans in farther. "If Greco finds out a Costa is working in the medical examiner's office, your badge will be revoked before you can type up a resignation."

I open my mouth, but nothing comes out. The horror of it crashes down in pieces. If he's right—and I know he is—then I'm not just at risk. I'm compromised. Bernardi sees it now. I'm a name he can use, a story he can sell. My bloodline makes me exploitable, my position makes me valuable, and the combination gives him everything he needs to control me. He knows it.

And now, so do I.

He studies my silence like it's the confirmation he wanted. "If you want to keep your job, your freedom, even your apartment, then you'll stop pretending you're some impartial little scientist. You're a Costa, whether you like it or not." He leans forward, voice dropping.

My pulse is everywhere. I swallow hard and sit straighter, but I don't say anything.

"You should think very carefully about what you're holding onto, Alessia. And who you're holding it for."

No longer able to sit there without breaking down, I slide out of the booth slowly, tossing enough euro notes on the table to cover my drink. As I'm walking, my hands are shaking so much I can't button my jacket.

"Don't wait too long to choose a side," he calls after me. "No one's neutral forever."

Outside, the air is cooler than it should be for late spring, and it cuts through the fabric of my blouse as I walk. The chill should help, but my body is already trembling from everything that happened inside the bar so badly that I have to lean against the lamppost just to steady myself. A Vespa zips past. Someone whistles from across the street. Rome is still alive, still lit, still bustling because life moves on.

But for me it has crawled to a stop.

I walk the rest of the way home, barely registering the buzz of traffic or the chatter from nearby cafés. One of Vincenzo's men follows at a respectful distance, never speaking, never drawing attention. He's a shadow to prove I'm not alone, though I feel like I am.

By the time I reach my building, my nerves are shredded. I scan the street again out of habit, then climb the stairs slowly, my hand still shaking as I grip the rail. The door to my apartment is ajar and it makes me pause.

The lock is untouched, not broken or bent—just left open. My stomach flips. But when I push the door open the rest of the way, I find Vincenzo on my couch, elbows on his knees, a drink in hand. He doesn't look up right away, just says, "I let myself in. Hope you don't mind."

I don't respond to him verbally. I shut the door softly, drop my bag, and cross the room without saying a word. I climb onto his lap, straddling him, knees pressed into the cushions on either side. My whole body is trembling as I drape myself over his chest and cling to his neck.

His hands come to my hips instinctively, steadying me. "Alessia," he says, voice low. "What happened?"

I shake my head, trying to form the words, but tears start, and when they do it feels like hell's floodgates have been opened.

Enzo waits patiently, smoothing my hair down my back, soothing me with coos and shushing me when appropriate. And when I've gotten enough of the emotion out to be able to articulate myself clearly, I speak.

"Bernardi knows," I whisper finally. "He knows I'm a Costa."

Vincenzo's jaw tightens. His fingers curl slightly against my waist as his eyes search my face, but he doesn't speak.

"He has proof," I add. "And he threatened everything. My license. My job. My apartment. Said he'd hand me over to Greco." I hiccup and sniffle, and he shakes his head in anger as he glares.

I watch his face contort as he realizes the new risk to me, the disaster unfolding before his very eyes.

"You're not going to deal with this alone," he says finally. "You hear me? Not one second of this on your own."

I nod, but the knot in my chest doesn't loosen. Because I know the next question will come, and I don't know how I'll answer it. What am I going to do now?

18

VINCENZO

The sun hasn't fully risen when I pull onto Via del Colosseo, but the city is already moving. Delivery trucks rumble past shops not quite open yet this morning. Someone sprays down a sidewalk with a garden hose, mist curling off the cobblestones. I sit behind the wheel of my car with the engine off, parked where I have a clear line of sight on the piazza. I sip burnt espresso from a paper cup and wait.

The man appears just after six thirty, dressed in a dark suit with conservative shoes and no tie—clothing that suggests a northern tailor unfamiliar with the pace and temperament of Rome. His steps are measured like he's counting the seconds between movements. He doesn't have the aimless energy of a tourist or the detached presence of a local officer. He isn't one of ours, either, and that makes him dangerous.

He loops the square twice before cutting across it at an angle that puts him close to the newsstand. His hand brushes the inside of his jacket twice, a subtle gesture that would mean nothing if I hadn't seen it a hundred times on the wrong kinds of men. He's checking the weight of something. Probably a piece he's not licensed to carry.

I've seen him before, maybe in Milan or Florence—one of the Bianchi enforcers who stays out of sight until something needs scrubbing. He isn't used for frontline work. He's a cleaner, the kind they only send when a mess is already guaranteed. The fact that he's here now, walking this route so early, tells me everything I need to know.

The Bianchis aren't monitoring from afar anymore. They're moving in for the kill. They're preparing for whatever comes next, which to them looks like a cleanup.

I pick up my phone off the passenger seat and dial a number I haven't used in years, speaking low and fast while I keep my eyes on the man outside. I keep my hand covering my mouth in case someone is trying to read lips. He picks up on the third ring. "Who the hell is this?"

"It's Enzo." The name alone should tell him who has the balls to call him, and I don't give any further explanation.

A long pause stretches across the line, just the sound of his breathing and distant traffic. Then, a gravel-edged voice answers. "You've got nerve, calling me."

"I wouldn't unless it was life or death. I need five minutes." My eyes stay locked on the cleaner... They call him Mr. Clean because that's what he does, but he looks nothing like the American detergent mascot.

"What's this about?"

"Gordo Costa, Detective Sergeant Elena Greco, and an old Palermo file. You're still working the internal access terminals, aren't you?" The cleaner moves again, carrying his freshly purchased newspaper and heading toward the downtown area on foot.

"That depends who's asking."

I glance up as the Bianchi cleaner stops at a café window and pretends to read the specials. "You owe me, Sal. Naples—remember? I kept

Luca Rizzo's name off your desk and his blood off the headlines. You want me to list the favors, or do you want to square one?"

Sal doesn't answer right away. I hear his breath scrape the receiver, followed by the clink of what might be a spoon in a coffee cup. When he finally speaks, his voice is tight. "Behind the *farmacia* on Corso. Twenty minutes. Don't make me regret it."

"You won't."

He hangs up, and I drop the phone in the cup holder and keep my eyes on the man across the square. He's still pretending not to watch me. That makes two of us. But I have somewhere to be now, and I'm not gonna waste more time on Bianchi shitheads if I can stop the bomb from detonating in the first place.

My contact meets me behind a pharmacy just off Via del Corso. He wears a leather jacket and a pair of faded jeans. His hat pulled low over his eyes shields him from unwelcome viewers, but I recognize him immediately. I park and slide out of the car, leaving my phone on the seat in case for some reason someone might get the courage to listen in on this conversation, and I jog over to where he stands leaning on the brick wall.

"You didn't hear this from me," he says, passing a folded paper under a discarded flyer.

I tuck the slip into my coat without looking. I didn't even have to ask him to dig, and the sap is already flowing. "I haven't heard a thing," I assure him, glancing back at my car and the direction I came from.

"Inspector Greco pulled an old Palermo case. It was sealed until recently, but she managed to dig it out and reopen it through a cross-jurisdictional claim. She's tying Gordo Costa to at least three syndicate killings—maybe four. That's the hook she's using to get around the statute and keep the anti-organized-crime case active."

My jaw tightens, but I don't interrupt. He shifts his weight, glancing toward the mouth of the alley.

"His daughter, Alessia's, name is on the witness list. She was the attending medical examiner on one of the old cases, and the lab timelines place her in physical custody of the evidence before it disappeared. That connection alone gives them leverage. They're calling it material involvement."

So that's the angle. They're not just building a case against Costa. They're constructing a noose around Alessia too. If they succeed, it won't matter that she's innocent. She's connected. They'll use that to grind her down until she breaks. "So why aren't they filing charges yet?"

"They're waiting for the smoking gun. I think they want Vescari. Maybe not... That's just my guess." Sal pulls the brim of his hat lower as a woman wearing a long blue skirt rides by on her bicycle, smiling at us as she passes.

I thank him and leave quickly, not looking back. He slithers back to wherever he came from, but I have the intel I've been needing. They don't have enough to actually press charges against Gordo or Alessia yet, and as long as she does as I tell her, she will be safe. It's just convincing her to do so.

When I get to the Costa compound, the tension in the air is immediate. Men mill around the perimeter, smoking and pacing with forced casualness that doesn't fool anyone. I spot Emilio through the map room doorway, hunched over a table with two of our lieutenants and an outsider I don't recognize. They're deep in conversation and don't look up as I step inside without knocking.

They're discussing hits, and not in the abstract. Real names are on the table—Elena Greco, Luca Bernardi, and Alessia. Emilio leans over the tactical maps like he's planning troop movement. His voice is clipped as he calls it a preventative measure. But it isn't strategy. It's a kill list.

He wants the problems erased before they spiral. To him, this is triage. Remove the infected tissue. Cut out the rot before it spreads. Alessia's name sits between the others like a stain he's already decided not to scrub clean.

I don't let them finish. "This stops now," I say, loud enough to freeze the room. "You don't get to take her off the board."

Emilio doesn't even look up. "She's compromised. We act, or we wait to be buried." The slip of paper burns a hole in my chest. If he would even stop and listen to me, he'd know how bad of a move this is. It's not something the cleaner can disappear.

"She hasn't given them anything," I snap. "She's trying to hold the line. And if you give me five minutes, I'll tell you why you're wrong."

He raises an eyebrow but says nothing. The others back off slightly, eyes darting between us. They know I'm crossing a line and the expression the newcomer gives me is nothing short of smug.

"Greco reopened an old Palermo file. She's got Gordo linked to three confirmed syndicate murders and possibly a fourth. Alessia is named as a material witness because she processed the evidence on one of those cases. That's all they need to start squeezing her." Red flags wave right in front of Emilio's face as his eyes grow darker.

"So you're confirming that she's a liability," Emilio says.

"No. I'm confirming that she's key. The case isn't solid until she testifies. Right now, she's still on the fence. You press her too hard, you force her hand."

He straightens, voice dropping an octave. "And you think the solution is what? Romance her into silence? Make her fall in line?" The dark laughter that erupts from his chest enrages me.

I grit my teeth. "I think the solution is giving her the truth and letting her see what's at stake. She knows the system and she knows how to erase the evidence. She's not a liability. She's an asset."

Emilio steps forward and the men back away. "We don't make decisions based on who you're fucking. You had your chance to put her in check, and now we do it my way."

"She's not a pawn," I growl.

"She's not special."

That's the end of it. I look at him—really look—and see the line drawn clear. Alessia's life on one side, the family on the other. He thinks this is the only solution and I'll never get through to him.

I turn and leave. The hallway blurs at the edges as I storm past Arturo, who moves to say something but thinks better of it. My pulse is a hammer in my throat.

Because now I know exactly what I'm up against. And I have to choose—follow my orders or protect her and take whatever comes next on my own.

19

ALESSIA

Morning light hits the countertop and glints off the subpoena beside my coffee mug. I read it yesterday and this morning, it's still there staring at me. The gold seal reflects a thin line of glare from the window. My name is printed in bold letters. The wording is plain and direct. I've been ordered to testify. My stomach tightens as I think through what that means, and I sip the coffee even though it's cold.

Chiara drops a spoon into the sink with a sharp clatter. She turns around, arms crossed, and leans on the counter behind her. In her scrubs she looks far more professional than her usual self, but the concern on her face is the same. She watches me with the kind of patience that has limits.

"You going to tell me what's going on now, or do I have to guess?" she asks as she taps her foot on the tile. The tip of her sneaker bobs and I return my gaze to the subpoena.

I set the mug down and lean into the counter. "It's work-related. A case I handled a few weeks back. Something's come up." My hand floats upward to rest on my neck, and I rub it unconsciously until I realize it makes me look nervous.

"Clearly," she says. "You look like you've seen a ghost."

I let out a slow breath. "It's tied to a 416-bis investigation involving organized crime. The review team flagged one of my reports, and now they think I either made a serious error or missed something important." The lies stream out of my mouth without restraint. It's not like I can outright tell her I'm hiding evidence or delaying a case because if I do, she's complicit and she could be forced to testify against me.

Chiara straightens. "Are they saying it's your fault?" The heels of her hands push against the counter behind her as her eyes flick to the notice and back to meet my gaze.

"No one's said that directly," I say, "but that's the implication. They're reviewing everything. I've been subpoenaed to testify. They want to know what I saw, what I missed, how I handled the report."

"But you didn't do anything wrong, right?" she asks. Her eyebrows dip in the middle as she shows how much she doubts my ability to be ethical. It sours my mood, but she has every right to doubt me and be suspicious. I'm doing exactly what they think I'm doing.

I hesitate. "I did my job. I followed procedure. But this is politics now. And if they think I'm covering for anyone, it could spiral." A knot forms in my throat and I start to feel a chill rising in my body.

Chiara drops into a chair. "So, what are you going to do?" She leans, adjusting the laces on her sneaker before reaching for her messenger bag. I know she has to get to work soon, and so should I. But the company this morning was a welcome change.

"I don't know yet," I say. "I can't ignore it. That would make it worse. It doesn't even matter if I quit, at this point. I still have to go testify. I'm sure it will be fine."

"You sure? Because it sounds like you're standing in quicksand." Chiara rises and slings her bag over her shoulder with a look of compassion. I'm sure if she could rescue me from this, she would.

"I am," I admit. "But if I run, I make their case for them. I have to face it."

She runs a hand through her hair, her expression tightening. "This sounds serious, Lessi. Like… life-changing serious."

"It could be," I say. "But I'll figure something out. I always do." My nonchalant shrug doesn't convince her and she narrows her eyes at me.

Chiara doesn't look convinced, but she nods. "You should get a lawyer. One with experience in this kind of mess."

"I will."

She clutches the strap to her bag and walks to the door. Her hand rests on the knob. "If you need anything, I'm here. I know I can't do much, but I can listen."

"Thanks," I tell her as she steps out the door and shuts it behind herself.

I've been nothing but a bundle of nerves lately, and anger rises inside my chest, only making that pressure build to the point of a searing pain. I feel like being destructive, as if smashing things will help me release some tension, but I don't want to smash my own things. So instead, I take the forged report out of the drawer, hold it over the sink, strike a match, and burn it. The paper curls and turns to ash, and I drop the last flaming bits into the metal of the sink.

I stay still until it's done burning and rinse the ash down the drain as I take our coffee mugs and rinse them out too.

When Vincenzo knocks, I've already tried to clean my face and regain my composure. I open the door and step back to let him in. He looks at me for half a second, then wraps his arms around me.

I press my forehead against his chest and the confession bubbles up before he even has the door shut. "I got a subpoena yesterday. If I tell the truth, my father will go to prison. So could I. They could charge me with obstruction, maybe even conspiracy. And if they find out how much you've done to help me, they might come after you too." I don't hold anything back because so far, Enzo has been the only thing holding me together.

"You should've told me sooner," he eventually says. His grip on me tightens, and I feel him press a kiss to the top of my head. "Emilio already thinks something's off. If he finds out I've been protecting you, I don't know how far he'll go. Why didn't you say something immediately?"

He's not acting surprised by this, so I assume he already knew it before I told him. But I don't bother asking him about it when I feel so rotten as it is.

"You had Rory here..." I narrow my eyes. "What were you doing?" I ask as I pull back just enough to look at him.

"I've been busy, that's all..." His stern expression tells me not to push, so I switch gears back to my own stress.

"What are we supposed to do? I can't lie under oath. I already falsified one report. If I go in and tell the truth now, they'll ask why I waited. I can't walk that back." Biting my lip, I think of how Dr. Bernardi has been pressuring me for so long to wrap up the Vescari case. I know when he sees me again, he will demand the report immediately. I'm not sure what to do now.

"It won't stop here," he says. "They'll dig deeper. Eventually, someone's going to connect the dots anyway."

"Exactly," I say. "We're both trapped. I can't expose my father without exposing myself. And you—"

"I knew the risk," he says. "You didn't ask me to get involved. I did it anyway. I'm just saying you have to protect yourself now. You're good to no one locked up." His hands slide up to cup both of my cheeks and he presses a kiss to my forehead. He's so gentle, it's hard to imagine that what he does in his free time is so horrific and unspeakable, he won't even tell me what it is.

We fall silent. The kitchen is quiet except for the soft hum of the refrigerator. I glance at the sink, where a few flecks of ash cling to the edge.

"I don't see a way out of this," I say. "There's no version of this where we all walk away clean."

Vincenzo reaches up and tucks a strand of hair behind my ear. "Then we figure out which version leaves the fewest scars."

Before I can respond, his phone vibrates in his pocket. He pulls it out, glancing at the screen. His expression tightens.

"What is it?" I ask.

He turns the screen toward me. A name glows across the top. *Gordo*.

My heart skips. "Don't answer it," I say quickly. "Please. What if he knows? What if he's calling to threaten you?"

Vincenzo doesn't respond. His thumb hovers over the screen as he stares at the name. The silence stretches, and I can feel my own breath quicken every time the phone vibrates.

"Enzo," I whisper. "Please."

He looks at me once. Then he presses the phone to his ear.

"Yeah?"

20

VINCENZO

I wait in the shadows beneath the overpass where the freeway splits and the sound of traffic blurs into white noise. This stretch of road never sleeps, and that's why I picked it. It's too public to be a trap and too loud for anyone to overhear us. A streetlight overhead flickers on and off like it can't make up its mind. My breath fogs in the air as I lean against the cold concrete pillar.

Gordo pulls up late, of course. He isn't careless. He's methodical. He was probably watching from a distance, might have men on every approach to make sure I came alone like he demanded. He scans the lot before cutting the engine and getting out. He's not wearing a coat, just a black sweater and gloves.

"You brought it?" he asks. He stops a few feet away, not reaching for the envelope until I offer it. His eyes flick from my face to the shadows around us, checking for trouble.

I nod and hand him the envelope. Inside, there are three printed photos, two audio transcripts, and a flash drive, each one carefully labeled and arranged—and I have duplicates of everything at home in my safe too.

He opens it and studies the contents without speaking. One of the photos catches in the wind, and he slaps it back against the others with a flat palm. His jaw works while he reads. The transcript outlines Greco's proposal to Luca—seize Costa property under the pretense of a corruption crackdown. The photos show meetings that weren't supposed to happen. One of them has a date stamp that matches the day Emilio met with the financial oversight committee.

"They're coming," I say. "Fast. If we don't pivot, they'll crush us." I shift my weight slightly, watching his face for any reaction. I haven't worked with Emilio's brother often, and I don't want to start now, but if Gordo is willing to help me keep Alessia out of hot water and Emilio isn't, I don't have a choice.

Gordo folds the documents back into the envelope and slips it under his arm. His face doesn't change. "It doesn't matter," he says. He shrugs like it's already out of his hands, a man resigned to whatever comes next.

I frown. "What do you mean, it doesn't matter?" I step closer, trying to catch his eyes. My body is so tight it feels like I might snap. If this fucker decides to give up the way his brother did, I will spill blood. A lot of it.

"I'm leaving Rome tonight for good. I'm done covering tracks, and I won't keep pretending it's not falling apart." He glances away, toward the freeway, like he's already halfway gone in his mind.

My fists clench at my sides. "You think your walking away fixes this?" I ask. I fold my arms across my chest, holding tight to what's left of my self-control, but my voice is sharper than I intend it to be. Gordo might not be my boss, but he's a dangerous man in his own right. I just can't fathom him walking out on his daughter.

"It doesn't fix anything. But I'm not dragging her down with me." He stares past me at the road, as if he sees something there I can't. His mouth pulls tight with something close to regret.

"Alessia?" I say. I already know the answer, but I need to hear it.

He doesn't look surprised. "She's all you want, right?" he asks. He tilts his head, waiting for confirmation. There's no emotion behind the question—just clarity. It's like he's washed his hands of her too. It sickens me.

"I'm staking a claim," I say. "I'm not letting anyone else call the shots with her." I keep my tone even. There's no apology in it, because I'm not sorry. She is mine now, and I won't let this family make her the scapegoat.

His expression hardens. "Then you'd better protect her—with your life, if it comes to that," he says. He points a finger at me, eyes narrowed like he's measuring my resolve. "You keep her out of this. That subpoena? Destroy it. Don't let her go to the hearing. Keep her safe."

"I already am," I say. I meet his stare without blinking. My stance is squared and solid, but I have no idea how to do what he's asking. I can't force her not to testify, and I can't make her destroy evidence, either.

For the first time, Gordo looks at me like he sees me clearly. He doesn't see Emilio's cleaner or Costa muscle. He sees someone else entirely.

He reaches into his pocket and pulls out a small brass key and a folded sheet of paper. "Take this. There's an account under an alias. It's enough to start over somewhere safe—for her. Don't use it unless you have to," he says. He holds it out like he's handing over the last piece of himself. His hand lingers until I take it.

My fingers close over the key, and our eyes meet. It's like he's transferring rights or something, which I know she'll never accept, but as a father, he's at least trying. That's more than he's done her whole life.

"What about you?" I ask. My voice is quieter now, the edge of my rage worn off. The question feels pointless, but I ask it anyway because I have to have an answer for her if she asks me.

"My fate's sealed," he says. "Hers isn't. Keep her clear of the family mess or none of what I'm doing matters." He shoves his hands back in his pockets. The conversation, to him, is finished. He's already turning away.

"Emilio's not going to let this go quietly," I say. "He'll see this as betrayal. He'll call you a coward." I take a step after him, needing him to hear it before he disappears into the night.

Gordo nods. "He'll want blood—maybe yours," he says. He glances back, the look in his eyes heavy with everything he's not saying. "I know how it ends for me. I just want her to be safe."

"He won't get it," I say. I speak with certainty, though I know the risk is real and closing in.

"Then be smarter than him," Gordo says. "Stay ahead of it. Cut ties where you can. And don't think for a second that you can save us both. You'll have to choose." He says it like a man who already made peace with the decision because he knows I have to choose his daughter. Even if we have to feed his name to keep her clean.

I look down at the key and the paper in my hand. The brass is cool against my skin, grounding me. "I already have," I mumble, but something in my chest tightens as I say it. There's no turning back.

He turns without another word and walks toward his car, climbs in, and pulls away without checking to see if I'm still watching.

I stay where I am, standing in the same place, carrying the burden of her safety in the palm of my hand. The key is cold, but the responsibility it carries burns hot in my palm.

I don't know how yet, but I have to find a way to protect her and keep this family from tearing itself apart. Gordo might be out, but the fallout he left behind is mine to clean up. And if I want Alessia safe—if I want any of us to survive this—I have to outmaneuver Emilio, outthink Greco, and find a path forward that doesn't end in blood.

Because the next choice I make could save her... or destroy everything.

21

ALESSIA

It's past three in the morning, and I've stopped counting how many times I've circled the apartment. The wine I poured an hour ago sits untouched on the counter and completely forgotten. Every light in the place is on, every blind is pulled closed, and every door is locked again. I check them compulsively, as if something might've changed in the last five minutes. It feels like paranoia is the inevitable result of living too long under this pressure.

Rory is stationed outside, which should comfort me, but it doesn't. The only thing I can think about is the fact that Enzo isn't here. The apartment feels hollow without him. Without Enzo, there's no conversation, no footsteps, no reassuring signs of life. It feels unnatural, not peaceful. I keep listening for something—anything—to fill it. But that alone is making me go mad with fear. Every tiny creak of the building makes me jump.

After what I overheard between my father and Enzo—my father demanding that they meet alone, his voice full of threats—I'm starting to understand what fear really feels like. It isn't just the kind that keeps you up at night. It's the kind that builds a nest inside your chest and lays eggs. It multiplies and spreads and turns every sound into a threat and every shadow into a monster.

Unable to sleep or even sit still without distraction, I log into my laptop just to distract myself, clicking through tabs I've left open. Then I check my email, not expecting anything urgent, just clicking mindlessly to keep my hands busy. My inbox is mostly clutter—promotions, updates, and spam messages. But one subject line stands out.

Compliance Required.

My stomach tightens instantly, a reflex I can't control, and I reach for the mouse to click on it and force myself to focus.

The message contains a single line of text.

Subpoena Update—Immediate Attention Required.

There is a PDF attachment, which I double-click on, and my stomach drops as the document opens. It's the same subpoena I received before, but this one is redacted, probably to avoid confidential information being stolen electronically. It lists the date of my court appearance.

The hearing is in three days. That means three days to cough up the report or decide to bury the facts. Beneath the court date, another image begins to load. My breath catches as I watch it render. The screen fills with surveillance stills. There are images of me and there are images of Vincenzo.

My mouth goes dry.

One image is from the alley near the lab, where I confronted him after he followed me. Another is from the pharmacy. A third was taken outside Rosa's apartment. Each is timestamped. Each one is invasive. They've been watching me for longer than I realized. And they haven't only been watching—they've been cataloging. This isn't random. It's strategic.

This is why Dr. Bernardi is pushing me so hard, because he's seen this shit. Someone knows the Costa family is leaning on me and they're going to force me to incriminate either myself or them. It's a horrible spot to be in considering whichever way I lean, I'm fucked.

I scroll through the images with trembling hands. At the bottom of the document, there is another note.

Failure to appear or submit an unaltered report may result in arrest and criminal prosecution.

My pulse stutters as I reread it. It's signed by Dr. Luca Bernardi, but it has Detective Sergeant Elena Greco's name on it too.

A chill ripples through me and settles in the base of my neck. My limbs feel heavy. My throat is tight. The implications are clear. There is no way out of this for me.

My first instinct is to slam the laptop shut. Instead, I grab my phone and scroll to Dr. Bernardi's number. It's three in the morning—he's probably asleep—but I don't care. I hit *Dial* before I can think better of it. My breath catches as it begins to ring.

There's a pause, confirming that I've woken him from a dead sleep, and he answers on the third ring, voice rough around the edges. "Leone?" His tone is level, but there's sleep behind it, and something clipped underneath that makes me stiffen.

"What the fuck is going on?" I hiss. Standing, I pace toward the window before stopping short and drawing back the curtain an inch. My eyes dart across the street as I try to steady my breathing. I can see Rory's outline near the car. He's not in the building where he's supposed to be, but that's okay as long as no one gets in here.

"I see you got my little reminder," Dr. Bernardi says simply. He's clearly groggy, his voice still catching on the edges of sleep, and I can picture him fumbling for his glasses in the dark. I've pulled him out of bed, jolted him from whatever thin layer of rest he managed to get tonight, and his calm tone isn't even slightly clipped, which makes it all the more disturbing. That, more than anything, makes my skin crawl.

"They sent me pictures of myself. Pictures, Luca. Who am I even working for? Why are you threatening me when I work for you?" My hand trembles as I let the curtain fall back into place. My skin prickles.

He exhales slowly. "You knew this was coming. DS Greco is moving forward, with or without you. She's confident you've manipulated your reports—and honestly, I think she's right. You were never going to play this straight." I can practically hear the shrug in his tone. It makes my blood boil. "Once a criminal, always a criminal."

"You don't get to act like this," I snap. My fingers dig into the base of the window frame as I grit my teeth. "I might share his DNA, but I'm not a criminal. I've done nothing wrong."

"Then be smart about it," Dr. Bernardi says, his voice still rough with sleep. "Figure out which side you're really on and act like it." His tone drops a register, as if he thinks saying it softer makes it more palatable, but his words hit me like a slap.

I don't answer him. I press the phone tighter to my ear, jaw locked. Every instinct I have is screaming to react, to push back, to yell or hang up. But none of that will help me. This isn't about what's right or wrong anymore. It's about staying ahead of whatever trap they've set. I need to be realistic, even if that means letting go of principles that separate me from the type of man my father is. No one's going to step in and fix this for me. I have to make the right call on my own.

His voice softens just slightly. "You have options. If you comply, the arrest warrant won't be filed. But if you don't..." He trails off, leaving the rest for my imagination to fill in. I don't need him to finish.

He doesn't say anything else. The line goes quiet, and the conversation is over now. If I don't do exactly what they want, they will steamroll me right along with my entire family. No one's going to intervene. I'm on my own.

I hang up without saying goodbye and toss the phone onto the couch, finally slamming the laptop closed. My heart is pounding hard enough to make me nauseous. My head spins. If Enzo were here, he would tell me that the choice is mine. He'd say that he will back me and that somehow, some way—even if it means using Costa resources and paying people to look the other way—he will get me out of this.

So I grab my phone again and type the message with shaking thumbs, the pressure behind my eyes threatening to boil over. My fingers move quickly out of desperation. I don't care what time it is. I just need to know he's okay—and I need to see him before I talk myself out of this.

Alessia: 3:14 AM: We need to talk. NOW.

I hit *Send*, then keep staring at the screen, willing those three little dots to roll over the screen indicating he's typing back. My chest feels tight. If he doesn't answer immediately, I'm going to lose my nerve. Because everything else already feels like it's falling apart.

22

VINCENZO

The hallway leading to Emilio's office stretches wide and pristine, lined with marble floors and quiet recessed lighting that glows softly on both sides. The floors shine with fresh polish, every detail curated to project wealth and control. One of the lieutenants nods at me as I pass, but I don't slow down. My jaw is tight.

I carry the paper and key Gordo handed me earlier, and my thoughts are already ten steps ahead. I don't care if the boss doesn't like what I have to say. He has to listen to me. No one has told me what his orders are concerning this entire situation, but given how he's washed his hands of Alessia already, I know I can't fight him. I'm only one man, and if he unleashes the Costa fury, I'll get put in a body bag right alongside Bernardi, Greco, and Alessia.

When I push into his office, Emilio is alone, hunched over a painting stretched out on his desk. It looks like one of the new ones his son's cash cow created. He doesn't look up right away, but I can tell he senses it's me. I'm the only one in this family with enough balls to walk into his office without knocking. Not even Victor does that.

I throw the paper and the key onto his desk hard enough that his whiskey sloshes when the key hits it. He lifts his gaze slowly, but I don't wait for pleasantries I know aren't coming.

"Gordo's gone," I say, watching Emilio's expression for the first flicker of reaction as his eyes narrow slightly, his hands still flat against the desk. "He's leaving town and washing his hands of Rome entirely. Bank accounts scrubbed." My eyes drop to the key as I shake my head at him.

I keep going without pausing for a reaction, unwilling to let him get a word in until I've laid it all out. I lean forward, planting both hands on the edge of the desk. "And Alessia is being hunted by them, Emilio," I add, straightening up just enough to gauge how deeply this hits him.

His eyes narrow as he flips the paper over, scans the numbers, and tosses it aside. "Then find her and end this," he says, but I can tell he's already written her off. His tone isn't angry—it's finished. Like she's a problem that doesn't need another conversation. "She wanted to play in this world. She made her choice. Let her deal with the consequences."

He brushes the paper aside with the back of his hand and picks up the key again, weighing it for a moment like he's deciding whether he even cares about the rest. Then he sets it down and finally looks at me.

His casual tone makes my skin crawl. I lock eyes with him and don't blink. "If she dies, the report still surfaces. They'll treat it like a silencing. You know what that means. Investigators swarming us, news crews parked on the street, Greco and Bernardi weaponizing every scrap of evidence. You want to talk about exposure? That's exposure."

He stands and walks around the desk. His pace is measured and slow, each footfall chosen like a predator closing in for the kill. "You think I'm going to let some forensic analyst sink this family? You think I can't find her precious files and remove them?" he snarls, shoulders pulled back as he towers in front of me.

"You should stop and think," I snap. "Because she's the only reason we haven't been charged already. She's sitting on evidence that can bury all of us. She's hidden it for now. And I'm the only one she still trusts." Red flags are going off everywhere. Emilio Costa doesn't fuck around, and I'm lucky he hasn't pulled his gun on me yet.

He stops in front of me, too close. "So, she's yours now? You take her side over mine?" he snaps, voice rising as he takes another step forward, challenging me with his stare.

"I'm taking the side that keeps us all alive. You want to gut the operation to prove a point, go ahead. But don't act shocked when the financial crimes unit freezes our accounts and investigators start dragging asses into court. We'll be lucky to get another few days."

He speaks more quietly, and there's a roughness to it that makes his frustration obvious. "She should be scared, not me. You think I'm losing sleep over this?" he says, rubbing the back of his neck like the pressure is finally starting to get to him. I see the cracks around the edges, though he will never show them. He knows I'm right.

"Then think like a man who wants to keep what he built. She's scared, yes—but if we corner her, she'll act out. Right now, I can still talk to her. I can calm her down, get her to hold off. Maybe she'll even make the report disappear. But if you make a move on her, she won't hesitate. She'll burn everything." My pulse is screaming past my eardrums because I don't know if I can actually make Alessia do anything. I'm living on two hours of sleep and a prayer to a god that may not even exist.

He turns and paces to his desk, stares at the painting like it might give him an answer. "I want them all gone," he mutters, dragging a hand through his hair as if saying it aloud might make it easier to accept. "Every shred of evidence destroyed. I want Greco and Bernardi, whoever else is involved—I want them silenced. And I want copies of her evidence as insurance."

As he turns to face me, I see his resolve finally weaken. He will do this as long as he has dirt on her to control her, but if my gut is right, hopefully, he won't need it.

"And you'll get all of that," I say, voice steady. "But not by killing Alessia."

"You're betting the future of this family on a woman who doesn't even want to be here," he says as he taps the top of his desk. Then he uses a finger to move the key as he purses his lips.

"No. I'm managing risk. She's the threat and the solution. You kill her, the report becomes a martyr's statement. You let me handle her, and we have a chance to bury this whole thing."

He doesn't speak for several seconds. The silence hangs between us while the decision settles into the room. He walks back to his desk, lowers himself into the chair with a tired grunt, and stares at the key I dropped. Finally, he speaks.

"You say she listens to you? Fine. Keep her quiet. Keep her away from anyone who can pull her in deeper. And keep my name out of her mouth," he says, "and never speak my brother's name in this office again. He's dead to me."

"Done," I reply, locking eyes with him one last time before walking over and tapping on the key. "This is payback, everything you gave him and more returned to you. He wants me to use it for her, and I'm offering it back to you."

I turn and leave him there, not waiting for a response, and I walk through the main hall toward the rear den, where a few of the younger men handle comms and errands. One of them is dozing on the couch, another scrolling through messages. I grab one of the new burners off the charging tray near the sideboard. No one asks what it's for. I slide it into my jacket and head for the back stairs.

As I descend, I pull the burner from my jacket pocket and unlock the screen. The glow lights up the stairwell in short bursts as I tap into my message thread with Rory, one of the only men I trust to handle this quietly.

Double Alessia's protection. No one gets near her without my say. That includes Bernardi or Greco.

I slide the burner into my pocket and push open the rear door, stepping into the courtyard. The air is cool, and the quiet finally feels like peace. No one's watching or listening. I stop at the far end, near the old stone fountain, and rest my hand on the edge while I think. My mind has been scrambled for days and I need the silence to make sense of this mess.

I need a plan. Something that doesn't involve more blood, something that protects her without tanking the rest of us. I've got ideas—half-formed and messy—but I know I'll need help. This can't be just me this time.

But the problem isn't only tactical. It's personal. Every time I go to her, I lose focus. She gets under my skin, scrambles my judgment, and I end up saying things I shouldn't, wanting things I can't afford to want.

My phone buzzes again—but not the burner. It's my personal cell.

I pull it out just as I reach the car, and the screen's lit up.

Alessia: 3:23 AM: We need to talk. NOW.

I stare at the message for a long second. She's not wrong. I need to talk to her as soon as possible, but I can't until I have my head on straight. Not without a plan in place, not when I'm still patching holes in this ship.

I type slowly to make sure I don't make any mistakes.

Vincenzo: 3:29 AM: I can't. Not tonight. Give me 24 hours. I'll come to you. It's time to do the right thing.

I send it and pocket the phone again, resting my hands on the roof of the car. I know what has to be done. And for the first time in weeks, I think I see a way through.

23

ALESSIA

I walk into the lab trying to act like everything is normal. I sit at my station and start logging slides, but my nerves are shot. Every time the door opens, I brace myself. It feels like they're coming to get me, and I panic. I keep expecting someone to call my name, to say they're here to arrest me. I force myself to keep working through the morning, reviewing chain-of-custody logs. I go through the motions because I have to, even though my hands aren't steady.

Rory walked me in this morning and didn't say a word about why Enzo wasn't around or why suddenly, he was right beside me instead of trailing behind me at a distance. And his silence said more than anything he could warn me about. I got the feeling he wasn't happy about his job of walking me to work, but I didn't ask.

I haven't heard from Enzo since the message now more than twenty-four hours ago. He told me to wait, so I'm waiting. But I'm barely holding it together.

When the elevator chimes just past noon, I know something's wrong. There's a shift in the room—it's subtle, but I feel everyone tense, even Dr. Bernardi. I glance up, already dreading what I'll see, and Detective

Sergeant Elena Greco walks in like she owns the place. Her hair is perfectly done, every strand in place like it was just set by a stylist. She wears a slate-gray suit and carries no trace of a smile. Her badge is clipped high, and she crosses the lab with her eyes focused on me.

She doesn't greet anyone, and Dr. Bernardi hardly looks up from his computer. Her presence alone does the talking. It clears the space around her like she's radioactive. If shadows could run away, I'm sure they would.

"Ms. Leone," she says evenly, stopping two feet from my bench. Her eyes scan the room once before settling back on me. She's already decided no one else in this room is of significance. "A moment." She tilts her head toward the hallway, expecting obedience without needing to raise her voice. That badge tells me I don't have a choice, so I sigh and push my stool back slowly and follow her down the hall without a word.

My pulse is thready, hand perched over the outside of my pocket where I can feel it vibrate if I get a notification. I want to call Enzo, but clearly, now isn't the time. She doesn't speak until we're in one of the unused conference rooms, the door clicking softly behind us.

"We've reviewed your case notes, every revision we've tracked so far." She remains standing, arms loosely crossed. Her stance makes it clear that she thinks this is a formality. That simply by showing up here with her badge on display, I will do whatever she wants.

I hold my neutral expression despite wanting to run away scared. "Then you know there's nothing conclusive yet." Steadying my voice, I place both hands at my sides to keep them steady, wiggling my fingers so they stop shaking.

She studies me like I'm a puzzle as her eyes rake over my face "There's plenty—enough to build out a timeline, evidence of foul play, and a link to the Costa operation directly." Her words are clipped and precise. She's not trying to persuade me at all because she thinks she knows everything. But the only way she'd know the facts is if I reported them, and I haven't. And no one else has touched that body but me.

My arms stay rigid at my sides as I study her face. Her lips flatten at the end of each statement like punctuation, her weight shifting slightly from heel to heel. She stays perfectly measured—the way a good detective should. She's already decided how this ends, and nothing I say will change it.

"Let me be clear," she continues. "I'm not here to pressure you the way Dr. Bernardi would. I'm here to tell you the facts. If you don't submit a final report by tomorrow, we'll proceed with obstruction." She touches her badge lightly like it needs to be straightened. The gesture is intentional, meant to signal authority rather than invite discussion.

My chest feels too tight in my blouse. I shift my weight and fold my arms. The move makes me feel safer, but I know I'm withdrawing.

"I haven't completed the tox panel rerun." I draw a shallow breath, trying not to show how cornered I feel.

She lifts her brows, unimpressed. "That's not what your timestamped data shows. You're stalling. And I know why." Her voice tightens slightly. She sounds like she's tired of pretending we're both professionals here.

I meet her gaze without blinking. "Then you should also know that tampering allegations go both ways." I meet her gaze without flinching, spine straight, though my stomach twists with the lie. No one has been tampering except me, and my words are baseless accusations, but I feel trapped.

Elena smiles faintly, but there's nothing warm behind it. "You think you're protecting your father. I get it. Loyalty's a complicated thing. But when the indictments come down, you're not the one they'll offer a deal to. He is." She speaks slower now, enunciating every word with careful intent, as if she wants me to remember them all. "He has the

Costa secrets and you're dispensable. Be smart, Leone. Don't throw away your career for this."

I feel the burn rising under my skin that makes it difficult to swallow. Fire boils in my blood, anger bubbling so deep in my chest and gut, I almost can't stop the screech of rage that demands to leap out of my throat in her direction.

She steps closer in a threatening move, but her tone is calm. Still, it leaves no room for negotiation. She's delivering a threat, not offering a warning. "Cooperate and survive, Dr. Costa. Or go down with him."

Greco turns toward the door and opens it. With a quick glance back at me to throw one more set of fiery daggers at me, she steps out and lets the door shut behind her.

I don't move for a full thirty seconds. My pulse is so loud it drowns out the air conditioning overhead. I stop thinking altogether. My body moves on autopilot. I walk fast, but not toward my bench. I head for the service stairwell at the end of the corridor and push the door open, stepping out.

The stairwell is completely empty, silent except for the faint echo of the door behind me. The air is cooler than the rest of the building, cutting against my skin and making it harder to breathe. I sit hard on the concrete step and bury my face in my hands, but no tears come, even though my body feels like it's collapsing inward. All I feel is pressure building in my chest, too much to contain. I can't find a way to release it.

I fold forward, elbows on knees, and try to breathe through it. I try to calm myself, but it isn't working. It won't work—not with everything closing in and no relief in sight. I don't have time to fall apart, but I stay frozen, unable to pull myself back together or stand up again.

I can't stay here. If I do, Bernardi will find another excuse to corner me, and I won't have anything left to give. I push myself up and slip out through the rear exit without signing out. The hallway's quiet, and I keep my head down and move fast.

Outside, Rory's leaning against the side of a black car, arms crossed. He straightens as soon as he sees me.

"I need to see Enzo," I say, pulling my suitcoat tighter around myself. "Right now."

He watches me for a second, then mutters, "You know he won't like that," as he turns and starts walking.

"I wasn't asking for your opinion. Besides, I've been more than patient." I'm not backing down. This man will take me to Enzo or I'll scream until he does.

He huffs. "You think you're the first person to blow up their entire life for that man?" He shakes his head as he pulls his phone out and starts texting someone.

"I'm not blowing my life up!" I snap. "I'm trying to stop it from burning to the ground." My throat feels like a boa constrictor is wrapped around it.

He glances sideways at me. "Honey…" His eyes roll, and I tense but I don't back down.

I shoot him a look. "If you've got something to say, say it."

Ignoring me, he continues texting and says, "I told him you were coming. Don't say I didn't warn you." And when he starts walking, I follow without hesitation, though I glance over my shoulder several times to make sure Greco didn't spot me and follow us too.

We round the corner to a parking garage entrance. Rory nods toward a spot tucked behind a concrete column, where a dark car sits with its lights off. He doesn't walk me all the way there, just jerks his head and says, "He's waiting."

Then he turns and walks away without looking back.

I approach the car slowly. Enzo's in the driver's seat, windows cracked, engine off. His posture is still, his eyes fixed straight ahead. When I reach the door, he doesn't move, but I know he sees me. I pull the handle and slide into the passenger seat.

Rory disappears, leaving us alone, but I don't feel like this is private enough for what I need to say to him. Somehow, it feels too exposed, like the walls have eyes and the instant I finally say what needs to be said, they will close in and I'll be dragged off to prison.

"It's time," I tell him, and he finally looks at me.

"I'm glad you realize that, Lessi. Because we're out of time." Enzo reaches for my hand. "But I have a plan. I just have a few things to handle first."

"You can protect me?" My chest is hammering. I'm about to do something I never thought I would ever be reduced to. Breaking the law is what my father and uncle and cousins do. It's not me. I walked away from the life my father wanted for me, and even though I was free, it sucked me back in anyway.

"Only if you trust me," he says, and I lean in, feeling too much pressure in my chest to do anything but cling to him.

He pulls me hard until I'm crawling over the center console as he slides the driver's seat all the way back. I straddle his lap and cling to his neck, sobbing, and he holds me so tight I almost can't breathe.

My breath hitches against his collar, but I don't pull away. Neither of us says anything right away. His hands rub slow circles on my back, grounding me even as everything else feels like it's falling apart. I press my face against his neck and sniffle, too afraid to let go of the only solid thing left in my life.

When I finally shift back to look at him, his eyes are on mine—like he's checking to see if I've settled or if I'm about to break again. His palm slides from the base of my spine to my hip, then rests there. The contact isn't rushed or possessive. It's steady, careful—just enough to tell me that he's claimed me as his.

"I shouldn't have come," I whisper.

"Maybe not... but I'm not sorry you did." Enzo's eyes bore through me, and I lean in and press my forehead to his. His hand moves again, to squeeze my side. His fingers inch the side of my blouse up, and I can feel the change in his breathing.

I reach down and loosen the top button of my blouse, and his eyes follow my movements. He kisses the side of my neck slowly, and I close my eyes.

I'm not thinking anymore, just feeling.

And when his hand moves again, I don't stop him.

Enzo's touch is feather light as he unbuttons my blouse one button at a time, his fingers skimming my skin with each pass. My breath catches in my throat, and I arch into his touch, seeking more of his heat. His lips trail along my jawline, sending shivers down my spine. I tilt my head back, inviting him in, and he doesn't disappoint. His lips brush against mine, soft and tentative at first, then more insistent as the passion between us ignites.

Our kisses deepen, tongues tangling in a desperate dance as our hands explore every inch of each other's body. I tug at his shirt, desperate to feel his bare skin against mine. He obliges, quickly shedding it before returning his attention to me. His hands skim up my thighs, bunching the fabric of my skirt before he undoes the fly of his slacks and pulls his swelling dick out.

Enzo's erection is hard against my center, and I can feel the heat radiating off him. My heart races in anticipation as he guides me down onto his length, one hand cradling my hips to position me. His other hand slides up my skirt, revealing the moisture of my desire. He groans low in his throat, and I arch my hips toward him, aching for more contact. His breath catches in his throat as he slowly pushes inside, filling me completely.

"Enzo," I moan, arching my back as he starts to move, thrusting in and out in a slow, delicious rhythm. His hands slide up my blouse, caressing my breasts, teasing my nipples until they harden under his touch.

He quickens the pace, driving into me with more force as our bodies grind together. The car rocks gently as I squeeze my thighs around his waist, drawing him even closer as we move in sync. The world outside fades away, leaving only the two of us and the primal need coursing through our veins.

As our bodies move together, I feel a familiar heat building low in my core. Enzo's thrusts become more urgent, his breathing ragged in my ear. I can't stop the whimpers and moans that escape my lips, the intensity of pleasure overwhelming any semblance of restraint. Enzo buries his face in my neck, muttering words I can't quite make out as his grip on my hips tightens.

My core begins to pulse, the first fingers of orgasm toying with my body. And when I jerk and twitch, he grunts loudly and bites down on my neck hard.

Finally, with a shudder and a muffled groan, he stills inside me, holding me close as our breathing slows to a less frantic pace. He doesn't say anything for a long moment, and neither do I. We just sit there, tangled in each other's arms, trying to regain control of our senses.

I'm still on his lap, breaths unsteady, my body soft against his. He presses a hand against the back of my neck, fingers threaded gently through my hair.

"You're coming with me," he says, his voice low.

I pull back just enough to meet his eyes. "Where?"

"First, home," he says. "You're going to pack a bag—just what you need. After that, I'm taking you to a safe house."

My stomach turns. "Why? What happened?"

He rubs a hand down my spine, not to comfort, but to steady me. "The Bianchis know you've been subpoenaed. They've decided you're a problem. I can't protect you if you stay at home."

I nod slowly, trying to swallow around the dry knot in my throat. The men following me, the ones trying to break into my home—it wasn't just intimidation at all. I'm scared. "What about the rest of it?"

"I'm working on it," he says. "I have an idea. It's not perfect, but if I can pull it off, it won't just keep you safe. It'll get us out of this entire mess."

He doesn't explain, and I don't ask. But I can see it in his face—whatever this plan is, it's already in motion. Maybe he's made calls or moved people. Maybe even taken risks I don't know about yet.

And if it works, it'll save me.

If it doesn't…

I'm too scared to ask what might happen.

24

VINCENZO

The container yard sprawls ahead in a crescent, surrounded by rusted fencing and iron skeletons of shipping crates stacked too neatly. This isn't a routine run. Emilio sent me here as some sort of quiet punishment for pushing back against what he wanted to happen. I keep my hand near my weapon, just in case, because my alarm bells are going off already without having seen a red flag anywhere.

It's supposed to be a quick exchange for me. I take the case of money and hand over a key and a note explaining where the weapons are stashed and get the fuck out of here. It's a new guy, someone Rory vetted, apparently, and Emilio doesn't feel great about it, but we can't pass up the opportunity to expand the business.

I kill the engine and sit still, one hand on the grip of my pistol. The cicadas are silent. There is no breeze to move the trees. No cigarette smoke rises from behind the containers. The yard holds its breath unnaturally. It feels abandoned, not just empty—like someone cleared it out and forgot about it.

The container marked with the large black numbers matching the ones on the memo indicating where I'm supposed to meet the contact is straight ahead. I walk toward it with the folder in one hand and the other resting near my weapon on my hip, expecting to pass the note and key off without hassle. I approach cautiously, scanning for movement.

The paint looks fresh, the metal too polished to have been sitting out here long. I draw my weapon as I step closer. The door is ajar, just enough to see that the lock has been cut clean. It swings slightly on its hinges, which I'm sure will squeak if I try to open it.

"Hello?" I call, expecting the contact to push open the door and walk out, but it stays quiet for a second. Maybe I'm a little on the early side, but I prefer watching them approach over being taken by surprise by someone waiting for me.

I pause ten feet back, crouch low, and scan the lot. Elevated scaffolding rises about twenty yards to the east. Another row of containers stands to the west, positioned with a clear line of sight to the water's edge. The space is a mess of rusted-out containers and scattered industrial debris. I can feel eyes on me, and the sharp burn of adrenaline in my throat makes my hair stand on end. Someone is out there, waiting.

I'm being watched, maybe since I got out of my car, and my stomach twists into a knot as I realize I should've brought backup with me. But I can't shy away from this job now.

I open the container door with my non-dominant hand, keeping my Beretta trained on the dark interior. The thick metal of the door shields my body as I take a few hesitant steps backward. I can't see into the container, but the flash of a muzzle has me jumping backward.

Gunfire erupts.

The bright flash blinds me for a second before my instincts take over. I dive behind the crate, rounds slamming into the metal just above my head. Shards of rust and paint splinter around me. The concussive pop of gunfire echoes off the container walls, deafening me, but I don't need my sense of hearing to fight back.

I roll and fire to lay cover as I try to retreat toward my car. A round connects with something—a scream follows, high and raw. One down. I get my bearings and pivot around the corner of the container with my gun high and aimed at them. With more than one shooter out here after me, I don't stand a chance. I have to get back to my car to safety before they close in and surround me.

A second shooter pops up from behind a stack of pallets as I shove the envelope with the key into my inner suit jacket pocket. I fire and hit the wood, splinters flying into his face. He flinches and tries to take cover, so I advance three steps, then drop as bullets slice through the air where my head just was.

Another shooter is above—perched on the scaffolding, maybe twenty feet up. He's got a scoped rifle and elevation. I fire twice in his direction. One round grazes his arm, sends him ducking behind the rusted rail. He returns fire, shattering a crate beside me. Wood flies up, peppering my chest and torso.

Then the flanker comes. I hear his boots crunch gravel from the right with fast, aggressive steps. He fires low and close, trying to pin me down before I can shift positions, but I manage to duck behind a drum and return fire, aiming for his center mass. The shot connects and he collapses, rifle clattering to the ground. His boots twitch once before going still.

Sweat rolls down my spine. My heart hammers so hard I can feel it in my teeth. My position is better than it was but still vulnerable. I've killed at least three of them, but I've counted at least half a dozen more guns trained on me. I have no choice but to run.

The one on the scaffolding is reloading as I break cover and sprint left, zigzagging through the shipping yard, ducking behind walls of steel. Another shooter shouts—maybe the one I clipped earlier—and tries to circle me.

"We got him! He's bleeding hard!" the man screeches, but I stop for nothing. He doesn't know I'm hunting him now.

I climb one of the containers, boots scraping on the rusted ladder, and come up behind him. He doesn't hear me until I'm there. One clean shot to the back drops him, and his weapon falls as he screams. I jump down, landing on him, and drive my elbow into his jaw hard. One point-blank shot to his temple and he stops screaming.

Grabbing his weapon, I sling its strap over my shoulder and keep moving. Gunfire erupts again from the left. At least four more shooters are closing in, cutting off my retreat to the car. I crouch and fire into the direction of the muzzle flashes, forcing them to scatter, but they're getting bolder now. They're not just holding the perimeter. They're hunting me through the yard.

A round tears into my upper arm as I pivot behind a stack of crates. The pain stuns me for a second. It's so hot, I feel like someone drove a fire poker through my bicep and I know I won't be able to lift a gun to shoot. I grit my teeth and keep moving, breaths shallow, legs pumping. I can't get cornered. If I slow down, they'll finish it.

I break into a sprint again, still zigzagging through the open stretch toward the fencing. Bullets hit metal behind me, but I see my car. It's my only shot. I dive for it, shoulder screaming as I crash against the door.

Hands slick with blood, I yank it open and throw myself behind the wheel. A round pings off the fender as I start the car and gun it. Gravel sprays behind me as the tires lurch forward, the car tearing through the fence. The chain link screams as it gives way and claws its steel fingers down both sides of my ride, but at least I'm safe.

As I hit the embankment, I spot movement in the mirror. A black sedan pulls into view in my rearview mirror—the same one I passed on the way in. That confirms that they weren't just lying in wait. They planned for a chase too.

I slam my foot to the gas pedal. The car jolts forward, the frame rattling as it hits a pothole and bucks onto the main road. Metal groans under the stress. The sedan cuts in fast behind me, its engine whining as it tries to gain ground.

My car isn't built for speed, but it has weight behind it. If it comes down to contact, I'll win. I speed onto a side road, hoping the tighter turns will force them into a mistake. The engine roars as I push it harder than it wants to go.

I spot a narrow lane and cut the wheel sharply to the right, rounding an old stone wall at speed. The sedan follows, but its turn is too wide. I brake hard and swerve, and my car slams into the rear quarter of the sedan, sending it spinning across the road wildly.

It hits a lamppost with a shriek of twisting metal. I don't stop to check whether the driver gets out. I push forward, eyes on the road, already scanning for the next threat.

My shoulder is throbbing, blood pouring from my arm, but I manage to speed off into the darkness and escape the would-be ambush the Bianchis clearly staged for me. When I finally reach the outer rim of Trastevere, my shirt is soaked and my side is on fire. I ditch the car behind a market, noting its location so I can send a cleaner to retrieve it. My legs feel detached, floating as I stagger down a side alley. The buildings blur, color bleeding into color.

I find a hole-in-the-wall bar to sit down for a second and limp in. A teenager wipes glasses at the counter. He sees the blood, the limp, the gun half-concealed in my waistband—and says nothing. But as I collapse into a booth near the back, he brings me a glass of some amber liquid I'm assuming is a stiff Scotch and a few towels with nothing more than a nod.

I pull my phone out with blood-slicked fingers and type:

Stay inside and don't text anyone. The Bianchis have started their strikes. I think they think you're taking everyone down.

When I hit *Send*, knowing Alessia will understand my message even though it's sent from a burner she doesn't recognize, I finally take a breath of relief. That was a setup, plain and simple. They're taking no prisoners now.

I pocket the phone, lean back against the wall, and breathe through the pulsing ache in my shoulder. Whatever this was, it wasn't just a scare tactic. It wasn't about stopping a weapons pickup. This was an attempt on my life because I got close to someone who is dangerous to all criminal organizations in this city.

And someone sent kids to do it.

25

ALESSIA

I haven't heard from Enzo in hours. This supposed "safe house" doesn't feel safe at all. Every bump in the night terrifies me. I've gone through half a bottle of wine waiting, pacing the tile floor, checking my phone every five minutes even though I know he'd call if he could. Something's wrong. I can feel it in my gut.

When the lock finally clicks, I fly to the door and wrench it open before he can and I find him standing there, leaning on the doorframe with a haggard look on his face.

He's bleeding.

There's a deep gash above his brow, and blood streaks down his arm where the fabric of his sleeve has been shredded. One hand is still gripped around the handle of his gun. But his eyes lock onto mine like I'm a sight for sore eyes.

"It's not as bad as it looks," he grumbles as he steps forward, but his knees buckle slightly. He's weak from blood loss, which I can plainly see, and I'm just glad the blood is on his sleeve and not his chest.

I slam the door shut behind him and catch him under the arm before he can fall. His jaw is tight. His skin is pale. The lock clicks as I twist it shut with one hand, and then I steer him toward the worn-out sofa.

My hands tremble, and my voice comes out tight with fear even as I try to hold it together. "Sit down. Let me take care of you." I lower him onto the couch, already grabbing the hem of his jacket.

"First aid kit is under the kitchen sink, I think." Enzo's words are breathy. I can tell he's in a lot of pain, but like most men of his caliber, he will never admit it.

He sinks into the cushions with a grunt and lets me peel the jacket from his shoulders. Blood slicks the side of his face and has soaked through his shirt so badly I can't see where the wound is. Rushing away, I grab the first aid kit from under the sink and return, dropping to my knees beside him.

"What happened?" I asked, trying not to let my hands shake too badly.

I grip the scissors from the kit and cut away his shredded sleeve to expose the wound properly, needing to see how deep it is. My mind flashes back to memories of my mother on her knees next to my father on nights like this. The bleeding isn't gushing, but it's steady enough to worry me. I press clean gauze to it and grab a sterile packet to prep the disinfectant.

"I got shot. What the fuck does it look like?" I can see on his face how much he's hurting, so I bite back my other questions, but I can't keep the grimace of fear off my face.

The wound runs straight through his bicep, which is very swollen, but the wound is clean enough to stitch if I can get the bleeding under control. I saturate a pad with antiseptic and press it firmly against the open skin. Enzo hisses through his teeth but doesn't pull away.

I clean around the edges first, then work inward, wiping away the grime and dried blood with slow, deliberate passes. My fingers are steady, but my chest is tight with panic. I don't know who did this and

I am afraid to ask, because I don't want to know how much worse this thing has gotten.

"My God," I mutter, more out of fear than shock. The gunshot is through and through, and it appears he hasn't nicked an artery. It will heal, but he could've died. Just six inches to the left...

When I've cleaned the arm thoroughly, I cover it with a square of gauze and wrap it up, then I toss the soaked pads into the waste bin and reach for another strip of gauze to deal with his face. He stays quiet, jaw clenched, trusting me to handle it. And he doesn't flinch while I clean the cut above his eye, though his breath catches when I accidentally lean on his arm.

He watches me the whole time. I can feel how heavy his mood is, like he's memorizing every move.

"You should've called me." My voice is sharper than I mean it to be, frustration crackling through the worry. He doesn't belong to me, but part of me wishes he did, that this wasn't some ginormous fuck-up that forced our worlds to collide.

"Didn't want to drag this shit through the phone." Enzo exhales hard and pushes my hand away, but I scowl at him and he relaxes to let me finish.

I tape the gauze in place and sit back on my heels and let my hands linger on his knees. "Talk to me, Enzo. Please."

He leans his head against the backrest of the couch. The shadows sharpen the angles of his face, and his voice drops low. "The investigation isn't our only problem now. The Bianchis want their connection to Matteo erased because they know if it comes out he's connected to them, we all go down." He lifts his arm, as if to reach for his face, then immediately winces and puts it back down, draped over his lap. I lace my fingers through his and wait.

My mouth goes dry. "So they want me dead?" I ask, confused. Don't they know if I disappear, Greco will just ramrod her way into my files and everything I know, they will know? Not to mention the fact that with my autopsy not finalized, they'll just put a different tech on it and everything will come out anyway?

His mouth opens like he might answer, but nothing comes. I search his face, and what I see there is worse than anything he could say out loud. It's not just exhaustion. He's convinced they'll hurt us both. I feel it hit low in my stomach, settling over me in a cold wave of terror.

"Emilio's only letting me keep you breathing because it protects the Costa name," he adds. "If you cooperate with the magistrate, you're alone. You'll have every crime family in Rome coming for you."

I stare at him, chest tight, then push up from the floor and walk to the window. It's pitch black outside, the yard barely lit by the porch lamp. The glass is cold against my fingertips as I brace one hand against the pane and stare out. "So, what's the plan?"

He exhales hard through his nose, shifting to sit up straighter. "I'll steal the evidence bag and swap the DNA. I've got access to pig's blood. Enough to corrupt what they pulled from under Matteo's nails. If the sample's tainted, it won't hold up in court."

"And the report?" I ask, still facing the window, though I already know what he's going to say. I can see his reflection in the window and watch him scrub a hand over his face.

"You're the only one who can do this, Alessia. You have to skew the findings or you're done." His voice is calm but firm, like he's already made the decision for both of us.

I turn slowly, arms folded. "And if I don't?" The idea of deliberately lying to the government, of falsifying evidence—it makes me sick in the stomach. I've officially stooped to the level of my father. I am a criminal, and there is no backing out now.

I turn to look at him as he says, "Then I can't protect you." The honesty in his tone slices through the last tether I have holding me to a life of normalcy.

For a moment, I can't speak. I can't even breathe. Because I know what this means. I'll lose my job, the only thing I ever earned on my own. I'll never see Chiara again—can't call her, can't explain. And my aunt, I'll vanish from her life without a word. I think of everything I worked for, all the years I tried to claw my way out of the Costa shadow, and now I'm right back under it. Worse, I'm complicit. I'm exactly what I swore I'd never become.

I walk to the couch and sit down slowly, hands resting in my lap. He leans forward, elbows on his knees, but doesn't speak. I think of Chiara, of the last message I never answered. I think of the keys to my lab still in my coat pocket and how none of it matters now. The weight in my chest is crushing, and no one can lift it, not even me. Enzo looks at me like he's bracing for me to fall apart, and I look at him, trying to figure out when I stopped resisting him and started falling in love.

"If it all falls apart," he says, quieter now, "I have Gordo's key. Access to funds, a way out. A house no one's touched since the seventies. It's off every map... And I'll go with you."

I study him. His shoulders slope forward from exhaustion. Blood crusts at his collar and stains the edges of his shirt. He looks wrecked—skin drawn, eyes dark—but he's upright. He hasn't given up on me, despite how hard I've fought him at times.

I slide off the couch, kneel in front of him, and rest my head against his chest. His shirt smells like sweat and gunpowder. I burrow my face into it and wrap my arms around him. "Ouch," he grunts, but I don't back away because now that I'm on his side of this war, he's the only thing I can count on.

His hand slides into my hair and he tangles his fingers in it. The touch is soft and grounding.

"If we survive this," I whisper, voice rough, "You're not allowed to leave me. Do you hear me?" Pulling back, I look him directly in the eye. "I don't think I can go back to my old life."

He lowers his head until his lips brush mine and he says, "I don't think either of us can."

I don't argue. I just stay there, breathing him in, knowing that whatever happens next—whatever it costs—this is the moment everything changes.

26

VINCENZO

The time for talking is over. We've stalled the magistrate, rerouted the threats, and bought Alessia enough space to breathe. But breathing is merely survival in this world—not really living. If there's any chance to clear her from the fallout and shield the Costa name from collapse, it starts here. The lab is where it begins. Matteo's body is the linchpin. The DNA under his fingernails is the risk. I don't care how crude it looks or how close it cuts. I'm going to make it impossible for anyone to prove what happened in that room.

"Van's moving," Diego says over comms, his voice steady in my ear. "Ten seconds."

I check my watch. It's 2:17. The van turns the corner at the end of the service road and rolls toward the rear loading dock with its lights low. Just like we planned it. I shift my weight behind the dumpster, eyes locked on the driver, while Nico positions himself above the dock scaffolding and Rory waits by the exit. We're in position to make our move as soon as the van stops. This job doesn't call for muscle. It calls for precision.

BEAUTIFUL EVIDENCE

"Positions," I say into the mic, my eyes scanning the dock. The van brakes quietly. Two fake orderlies in scrubs—ours—hop out and look around, one pulling out a clipboard while the other taps on his tablet. And we walk straight up to the van like we've done this a hundred times.

"You really got three of Emilio's guys on the manifest?" Nico asks under his breath as we approach. It cost us a hefty sum, but I made it happen.

"Pulled them from his private crew," I say. "Swapped two into the night shift rotation last week and bribed the route supervisor for the third. He thinks he's doing a delivery to state storage. He has no idea who's in the bag."

Nico gives a low whistle. "You're getting good at this, *compare.*"

"Too good," I mutter, stepping up just behind the van as our fake orderlies open the back doors for us.

I climb into the van before anyone else, nostrils flaring at the sharp smell of bleach and disinfectant. The dome light inside flickers overhead as I step up beside the stretcher. Matteo's corpse is zipped up in a sterile body bag, the tag hanging limply from the zipper pull. His body looks worse in the dim light, slack and gray, like he's a floater who's done bloating. There's no time to dwell on it.

I unzip the bag halfway and snap on latex gloves as Nico passes me the tools. Vescari's fingernails are caked with dried blood and grime. Lab swabs won't miss that. So I take the brush and scrub the nail beds hard, foam and peroxide mixing into pink suds as I go over each finger. I don't take shortcuts. One missed spot could take us all down. My gloves are soaked when I finish, but I don't slow down.

"Syringe," I mutter, reaching my hand out. I glance up the alley and see it empty. This time of day is a risk, but we weren't able to convince them to transfer the corpse at a different time.

Nico hands it over. I draw the pig's blood and inject it into the soft tissue under each nail. The trick isn't volume—it's contamination. If the lab gets one good sample, we're screwed. But if every swab's dirty, every result is garbage. The blood seeps out slowly around the nail beds as I work. It's crude, but it's effective.

"Three minutes," Diego says. "Driver's ready to roll."

I finish the last injection and wipe the fingertips dry. Matteo's hand flops back onto the stretcher, lifeless and ruined. Before I zip the bag, I grab the blade from my pocket and lift the sheet just enough to see the carved symbol on his stomach. It's deep—clearly deliberate—and anyone who recognizes it will know exactly who left it there. I drive the tip of the knife into the mark and drag hard across it several times, turning the shape into a shredded mess of tissue. It's not enough to hide what was there completely, but it will stop anyone from being sure.

Then I zip the body bag shut, tag it with the altered numbers, and nod at Diego before handing Nico the syringe and knife. The driver climbs in. Our guy signs off with the forged timestamp and nods like nothing happened. The van pulls away from where we stand watching, with Matteo's body in the back and no one the wiser.

I stay where I am for a moment, watching the taillights vanish into the curve of the street. It should feel like relief. But all I can think about is whether she'll be able to do her part. She's not like us. She didn't grow up inside this world. She was on the periphery, and barely at that. What I just did—what she'll have to do next—isn't something you come back from. If she freezes, if she hesitates, it'll all unravel.

"You think she's ready?"

I turn to see Rory beside me, hands stuffed in his jacket, watching the van disappear. He doesn't sound skeptical. Just curious.

"She doesn't get to be ready," I say, eyes still on the curve where the van disappeared. "None of us do."

Rory pulls a pack of gum from his coat pocket and offers me one. I shake my head, and he pops a piece in his mouth, chewing slowly as he watches Nico and Diego stroll off toward the side alley, jackets loose and hands deep in their pockets. No urgency now. The job's done.

"Those two make it look easy," Rory says, nodding toward them.

"They've done worse," I answer. "This? This was clean."

"Yeah, well," he says, rocking back on his heels, "clean jobs usually mean dirty follow-ups."

He looks over at me, jaw working. "You really trust her to do this?"

I take a breath through my nose and finally glance away from the street. "She's not stupid. She knows what's at stake. I'm not worried about her skills. I'm worried about her conscience."

Rory lifts an eyebrow. "You think she'll crack?"

"No," I say. "I think she'll carry it. Even if no one else knows what she's done, she will. And that's a different kind of damage."

He gives a low whistle, then nods like that settles it. "Guess we'll find out."

I slide into my car across the street and dump the gloves in a burn bag under the seat. My hands are still shaking from pure adrenaline. It's a rush to do what we do, but I have a feeling Alessia is going to be shaking too, for an entirely different reason.

If she pulls it off, we're through the worst of it. I keep thinking about what that might mean—what kind of life we could build in Rome once this is buried. She could go back to medicine, if not in the public eye, then behind the scenes. I could step out of the shadows without stepping away from the family. Start running things cleaner. Cut out the rot before it spreads. There'd still be danger, still be blood, but we'd be building something that lasts. A future inside the world we were born into—but on our own terms. But none of it happens unless she gets through tonight.

Vincenzo: 2:59 PM: My part's finished. You're up.

I stare at the screen for a second before locking it and sliding the phone into the center console. There's nothing else to say. If she can hold the line like I did—if she can get the paperwork filed and the sample suppressed—then we might actually survive this. She's smart enough to rewrite the rules. I just have to hold the door open long enough for her to walk through.

27

ALESSIA

The cursor blinks against a white screen while I sit frozen, index finger hovering above the keyboard. The login screen waits for my credentials, the same ones I've used for years. I type them in like it's any other morning and I'm not about to erase the truth.

The system loads slower than usual, and the pathology records come up in a list. I scroll until I find it—Matteo Vescari, case code 411-23. My pulse jumps when I click in. I half expect an alert to flash, a firewall to trigger, something to block what I'm about to do. But the software obeys me like it does every day.

That's what makes it worse. If there were friction—if the system pushed back, stalled, flagged something—it might feel harder to cross the line. But everything responds like it always does. It feels too easy, and that ease makes me sick.

The guilt creeps in quietly, not because I believe my father deserves justice, but because I know how hard I worked to earn this access. I was proud of it once. I believed in rules and records, and now I'm the one dismantling them.

Everything is in place. The histology files are logged. The toxicology report is clean. The scene photos are labeled, and the autopsy notes are stored in sequence. I skip to the forensics tab and pull up the DNA record—Chain Sample #84723. It's the record tied to the blood under his fingernails. It's the same one that pointed straight to my father.

I open the metadata and disable the visibility layer. Then I run a permanent deletion script. It prompts me—*Are you sure?*—as if this is just any other misfiled sample.

I click *Yes*.

Then I close my eyes for a second to will away the shame I feel. When I open them, the screen refreshes and the link vanishes. I run two more commands to clear cached data, then wipe the shadow file. All backups are erased. Every reference log and lab flag is deleted.

But that's not enough. I know the protocols inside and out. I know how to bury things so deep they'll never resurface—but it still feels like painting over rot. I picture what will happen if someone decides to dig anyway. What if they request an audit? What if someone reopens the case out of spite or curiosity? What if someone else I trained with starts asking questions I can't answer without giving myself away?

That fear keeps pushing me, harder than guilt ever could. So I do more. I rewrite the input fields manually, changing the record type to read, "*Sample degraded. No viable DNA sequence obtained.*" Then I scrub the timestamp and inject a false string of lab attempts so it looks like we tried to rerun it. That's the part that will get the right eyes off my back. It won't trigger any supervisor flags. It won't get sent up to the magistrate.

When I'm done, I sit back and stare at the empty screen. My hand drifts to the mouse again, fingers trembling. I open the print menu and send the modified report to the lab printer. The hum and whir of the machine feels too loud in the sterile quiet, and I feel accused and judged too. I pull the paper from the tray, still warm, and skim every word again.

Degraded sample. Secondary attempts unsuccessful. Inconclusive.

I sign it with a trembling hand, and my heart is beating so fast it makes my teeth hurt. I slide the sheet into a folder and head for Records.

The hallway outside is washed in sterile light that feels bright enough to expose everything. I keep my head down and move quickly. I know the security cameras are on so I keep my steps even, and I don't look around.

Downstairs, I log the file into the central pathology cabinet and sign the transfer register. The nurse at the desk barely glances at me. The nurse doesn't say anything. No one looks up. I nod once, careful not to draw attention, and turn away with steady steps.

Back in my office, I shut the door and twist the lock, then cross to the desk and open the drawer with the encrypted USB. I plug it in and access the hidden file structure. Inside, the folders contain temp logs, timestamped edits, audio clips from the initial exam, and scanned images of handwritten notes. Everything I used to build the case. Everything that could unravel what I just did.

I delete them all, one folder at a time. The screen flashes with progress bars as each section vanishes. I wipe the drive three times before removing it, wrapping it in a paper towel, and snapping it in half. The metal splinters and the board cracks down the center.

I toss the pieces into the trash can, cover it with files from the recycling bin, and sit at my desk, breathing through my nose. My heart is hammering and I feel like I may start crying any second.

This is it. It's done. I can't undo it, and I can't change my mind now.

I also can't get out of the testimony I'm expected to give in front of the deposition board and Dr. Bernardi, where Detective Sergeant Elena

Greco will grill me and I may very well crack. That thought makes my stomach churn and I want to reach for my phone to call Chiara, just to hear her voice. I'm going to miss her so much.

Instead, I check the burner phone in my jacket pocket. There are no new messages. The screen remains blank.

My task is complete. Now all I have to do is leave and meet up with Enzo and pray everything plays out the way he said it will.

My stomach knots. The tension doesn't come from guilt. It comes from something worse. Guilt fades over time, lessens as time passes. Fear doesn't.

If anyone catches this—if anyone traces a single string back to me—I won't just lose my job. I'll lose the protection that comes with it and I'll go to prison right alongside hundreds of criminals who will be standing in line next to my cell to punish me.

But if Enzo did his job, then the truth no longer exists in any form— no paper record, no digital file, no official archive, and no shred of physical evidence linking Gordo Costa to the murder.

It exists only in my memory.

28

VINCENZO

It's been a week since the ambush, five days since we ran the body swap, scrubbed the DNA, and bought ourselves time with a falsified report. Alessia hasn't been back to the lab since and I haven't pushed her. The pressure's cooled, but a strange silence between us has taken the place of the superheated tension and I'm not sure how to feel about that.

I still have men watching her apartment, but not even Dr. Bernardi has attempted to approach her. The Bianchis have backed down, and all that's left is for her to attend the deposition for which she got the subpoena, and her life will be clear of any ties to her father's. Except the soul ties which I know will haunt her.

I knock once before unlocking her door with the key she gave me weeks ago. The deadbolt sticks, same as always. I step inside and close the door behind me without calling out, but I know she's expecting me. Somewhere inside the apartment, I hear the low scrape of cardboard shifting against the floor.

I follow the sound until I see her on the living room floor, surrounded by half-filled boxes and stacked folders. She doesn't look up, but I know she hears me. She's stacking lab notes and framed photos into an open box. Another box sits beside her, already half-full with coats, boots, and the disassembled parts of a French press she probably won't need again. The curtains are open and light spills across the floor, catching on the tape dispenser beside her knee. The sharp metal edge glints under the sunlight.

I step forward slowly and let the door click shut behind me. "You moving out?" My voice sounds too casual, but I don't know how else to start this conversation. Emilio has ordered me to pull my men back now. The risk to us is over. With Alessia's help, we managed to destroy any ties Gordo left between us and the murder victim, and he won't waste resources on making sure she's okay following the deposition.

But I'm not ready to give up on her personally. There's too much left unsaid between us.

Alessia doesn't look up. She slides another folder into the box and says, "Not exactly... Maybe... I don't know." Her tone sounds defeated and reserved all at once.

I move toward her and lean one shoulder against the wall as I stare at the stacks of evidence to the contrary that surround her. "Then what is this?"

She sits back on her heels and rests her hands on her thighs. "I'm not going to have a job when this ends. I might as well be ready."

I cross the room, take the envelope from my coat, and set it on the table next to her half-empty coffee mug. She looks at it, but her hands stay on her legs. She raises her chin slightly. "I don't want your money, Enzo."

I stay standing next to her as I sigh hard. "It's not mine. It's Gordo's money—or part of it—what he left behind. You're owed this. There's more coming." The decision to take care of Alessia financially was always mine to make. Emilio washed his hands of his brother permanently, and he was prepared to let the money sit in Gordo's off-shore account and never touch a dime of it. It rightfully belongs to Alessia now, and I'm going to see to it that she gets it.

Alessia exhales through her nose and scrubs her hands over her face. Her gaze stays fixed on the ceiling like it might offer some kind of answer. "You think a payoff changes what I did?" I see every worry line on her face, the taut way her shoulders fill out the blouse she's wearing. She's a fighter, but everyone has their limit. I can see she's reached hers.

I lower myself to the floor across from her and sit with my legs sprawled out and my shoulders hunched. "No. I think it buys you space to figure out what comes next." Money isn't the answer, but it can provide relief when we need it most. In her case, it might provide more than relief if she lets it.

She draws one knee up and wraps her arms around it. Her voice drops to something quiet and tired. "There's nothing next, Enzo. Not in that job. Not in any lab that expects clean hands. I'm done here. I won't work in Rome again, maybe not even in Italy. If I don't get fired, I'm quitting. I can't do this job knowing at any point, the criminal underworld will squeeze me like this again."

I shift one of the boxes out of the way and rest my arms on my knees. "Then stop letting that place define what you do."

Alessia lets out a dry laugh, but there's no smile on her face. "That simple, huh? You think walking away from forensic work is like taking a vacation? I've spent years trying to believe science could stand up to politics. Turns out, I was wrong."

"You don't owe them anything," I say, and I mean it. Her loyalty's been stretched past breaking, and I see the will to fight slowly fading away in her eyes.

She doesn't answer at first. The light shifts across her face as a cloud moves past the window. Her expression tightens—not with anger, but with clarity. "I stayed because I thought I could do good. That's the only reason I ever took the job. But I was wrong. My father's legacy is too big to ever get away from it."

I reach for her hand. She doesn't flinch. She lets me take it, and I pull her until she comes closer, climbing onto my lap.

"You're not that person," I say quietly. "You never were." My hand smooths the hair off her face as she settles into my embrace. It's a hard thing watching her spirit not fight back anymore. The part of her that is most precious is the part that seems like it's dying, and I feel fully to blame for that.

Alessia's voice thins to something raw. "I will be if I stay. Maybe not tomorrow. Maybe not next month. But eventually, I'll lose the part of me that still cares. The second I stop flinching at a cover-up or lying to a victim's mother, that's it. That's the end of the line."

Wrapping my arms tightly around her waist, I hold her to myself as I say, "Then let me help you find something else."

She snorts. The sound isn't mean, just tired. "Doing what? Teaching chemistry to bored rich kids? Selling skincare supplements to influencers?"

I shift under her and readjust her position on my lap, then reach up and push her dark locks behind her back. "Come work for me." The solution sounds simple to me, but I know it won't be that easy for her to accept.

That gets a laugh. Alessia picks up a roll of tape, spins it once in her fingers, then sets it back down. "Doing what? Helping you catalog which bullets deform in lake water? More cover-ups? More evidence to destroy?"

"No," I say. My jaw tightens at those words, but I know she doesn't mean to be so cynical. "Helping me make something of your father's legacy and keep your uncle out of hot water."

She finally looks at me full-on. Her eyes are skeptical but alert. "You're serious. You want me to pretend I don't know what they do?"

I nod. "You don't have to work for me. You don't even have to touch anything illegal. But you could consult as an outside specialist. You'd keep your title, your autonomy, and your ethics. Maybe it's called clinical oversight in your field, or best practices review. Whatever the terminology, it means setting standards and watching the line—something you've always done anyway. We'll keep it separate from what I do with the rest of the business. Keep yourself clean. You'd be helping, not hiding anything. And you'd be with me. We wouldn't have to split our lives down the middle just to be together."

Alessia looks down again. Her voice softens. "You're talking like we get a future." Her fingers toy with the top button of my shirt. I see how she's chewed her nails down to the quick, and I clasp one hand and bring it to my lips to kiss it.

She doesn't resist, but she's tense at first. I wrap my arms back around her and wait. Her head drops to my shoulder after a few breaths.

"You think I don't know what my father was? What I've been?" I ask. I don't want to say it out loud, but there's no dodging it anymore—not with her in my arms, not after what we've survived. I've lived my entire life operating on necessity, not desire, and now I'm admitting that it isn't enough. That's the weight I feel—finally choosing something for myself, knowing it might cost me everything else.

Alessia stays quiet, but her hands press lightly against my chest. Her body is rigid in my arms, and I press a kiss to her cheek. Somehow, in the middle of all this shit fight of a life, I found someone I can be with and not have to keep my guard up. I can't let that go, but I won't force her to choose me. She has to do it because she wants me.

"I'm not proud of it. But I did it because I thought it was necessary. I thought being smarter, faster, colder than the next guy was the only way to keep people safe."

She tilts her head slightly. "And now?"

I close my eyes for a beat. "Now I think survival's not enough." I shrug a shoulder as she leans into me, and I tighten my hold around her. "You can't build something real if you're always planning how to cut loose. And you can't keep a woman like you at a distance and expect her to wait."

Her breath catches. She doesn't pull away. "I don't know how to be with someone who lives in your world. Someone who moves through it like violence is currency. Someone like my father..."

"I don't know how to be anything else," I admit. "But I know what I want, and that's you."

Her fingers curl around my neck, though her grip is uncertain.

"I'm not promising anything, Vincenzo," she says after a while. "I don't know what this is or what it becomes."

I rest my chin lightly against her temple. "I'm not asking for a promise. I'm asking if you can picture a version of this that doesn't end here, right now." She has to feel the way my heart is hammering. There are a hell of a lot of things that get my blood pumping, but nothing scares me. Nothing except the idea that she'll walk away and I'll never see her again.

Alessia doesn't speak for a long time. When she finally turns her head and looks up at me, there's nothing performative in her expression. "I could tell you all the reasons this is a terrible idea," she says, her tone almost wry.

"Please don't. I've already rehearsed them." I grin and fight a chuckle, and she smiles softly too.

She lifts her hand to my jaw, studies me for a second, then kisses me. The kiss lingers without urgency, no theatrics or hesitation, just the steady, honest weight of a decision made. When she tries to back away, I deepen the kiss.

One hand slides higher up her shirt, fingers finding the warmth of her skin underneath. She doesn't pull away. Instead, she presses closer. Her tongue dances with mine, testing and teasing, before she nips at my bottom lip. I growl low in my throat and deepen the kiss, my other hand molding to the curve of her hip.

As much as I want this, want her, I force myself to move slowly. To savor each touch, each sensation. My fingers drag over the lace of her bra, tracing the outline of her nipple through the fabric. Her breath hitches, and she moans into the kiss. The sound sends a jolt through me straight to my groin.

Alessia's hands make their way to my belt, deftly unbuckling it. I groan as her hands slip inside my trousers, wrapping around my hardening dick. She bites her lip and smirks at me before licking my lip and using her teeth to rake over it.

"Is this part of your plan, Mr. Morelli? You pull me onto your lap and get me worked up, then fuck me until I'm whimpering your name and that makes me yours indefinitely?" Her tone is playful, and I growl into her mouth as she kisses me.

"Well, Ms. Leone," I murmur, careful to use her chosen name rather than her given name so I don't sour the mood, "if it works, why fight it?"

With an impish grin, I stand up, gripping her hand to haul her to her feet. She stumbles into me, her breasts pressing against my chest, and I wrap my arms around her waist to steady her. "I think we need a more... private location for this conversation," I say, my voice low and husky in her ear.

Alessia's cheeks flush a delicious shade of pink, but she doesn't protest as I lead her down the hallway to her bedroom. The room is dimly lit with the curtains drawn, casting everything in a sensual glow. My heart pounds in my chest as I kick the door shut behind us, locking it for privacy. I don't want anyone or anything interfering with this moment.

The low lighting casts enticing shadows on her flushed skin, and I can't help but admire the view. "I've been waiting my whole life for someone like you," I confess, my voice raw with desire. I rest my hands on her hips and lean into her, ready to take her against this door.

She licks her lips, a playful glint in her eyes. "You're not the only one, Enzo." She reaches for the hem of her blouse, lifting it over her head to reveal the lacy bra beneath. My vision clouds with lust as her full breasts spill free. I groan under my breath, unable to tear my eyes away.

"You're so beautiful," I gasp, my hands trembling as I fumble with my own buttons.

Alessia smiles up at me, her expression a heady mix of desire and vulnerability. "I'm glad you think so." Slowly, she unhooks her jeans, letting them slide to the floor and revealing a pair of matching lace panties. My heart pounds in my chest as I drink in the sight of her, so breathtakingly sexy yet vulnerable at the same time.

"You have no idea," I manage to say, my voice rough with need. I shuck my shirt off and undo my trousers, letting them drop to the floor along with my boxers. My erection strains between us, and Alessia's gaze flickers downward before meeting mine again, her cheeks flushed but her eyes filled with determination.

"I want to be with you so bad, Enzo," she whispers, her voice barely above a whisper. Her admission emboldens me, and I grip her hips, lifting her onto the edge of the bed. She gasps, but her eyes darken with need, and she wraps her legs around my waist.

I groan as our bodies press together, her heat against my length igniting a fire in my veins. "Tell me what you want," I growl, nipping at her neck as I fumble with the clasp of her bra.

"I want you," she pants out, arching her back to give me better access to her collarbone. "I want to feel you inside me, Vincenzo. I want to have a future with you." My teeth sink into her skin, and at the same time, she shoves her panties down over her hips.

Lying back, her body pulls away from mine, but only so she can remove her panties, and then I'm between her legs, finding her sopping center. My hands struggle to undo her bra and she rescues me, and then there is nothing between us but her slick moisture.

I groan, the sound guttural and primal, as Alessia's delicious wetness coats my fingers. The slickness between her legs proves her arousal, and I can't help but grin. "You're so wet for me, *Bella*," I growl before lowering my head to taste her nectar. Her flavor explodes on my tongue, sweet and salty, driving me further into the depths of lust.

Alessia moans loudly, her hands gripping the sheets as I lap at her core. Her hips buck against my mouth, urging me to go faster, harder. I oblige, and my tongue dances over her swollen clit. Her scent fills the air, musky and intoxicating, spurring me on even more.

Alessia's moans become more urgent, her hips bucking faster against my mouth. I know she's close, and I don't want her to come like this. Not without me inside her. Reluctantly, I raise my head, my face glistening with her juices. I meet her gaze, and what I see there takes my breath away. Trust. Desire. Love.

"Enzo," she pants, her hair a tangled mess around her flushed face. "I want you inside me now."

I can't deny her anything in this moment. With a growl of pure need, I line up my throbbing dick with her slick entrance and push inside her. Her heat constricts around me, and we both moan in unison as our bodies become one.

Alessia's nails dig into my back as she arches her hips, taking me even deeper. "Enzo," she gasps, her eyes fluttering shut. "Oh, God, Enzo."

"I've got you," I grunt, gripping her hips and starting to move in slow, deep thrusts. "I'll always have you, Alessia."

"Oh, God, please…" Her words are a balm to my soul, soothing the rough edges of our past week apart.

"I've missed you," I whisper in her ear, my hips picking up speed as she moans my name. Her nails claw my back, and I know she's close. I can feel her pussy clenching my shaft. I want to feel her come apart in my arms, to know this is real, that we have a future together.

Her legs tighten around my waist, her body arching off the bed as her orgasm crashes over her. "Enzo!" she cries out. She's frantic, gasping and grunting as she convulses. I bury myself deep inside her, as deep as I can go, feeling her pulse around me.

The moment feels magical, like something between us has shifted, and I don't have to think about her leaving at all anymore.

I pump slowly in and out of her as my release fills her and drains out. Our lips find each other again, and I push the hair off her face as I open my eyes to look down at her.

"I love you, Enzo…" She's winded and her voice is breathy, but it's the most beautiful thing she's ever said to me.

"You're mine, Lessi. Now and forever." And I mean it. I'm never letting this woman go, no matter who I have to fight to keep her in my arms permanently.

29

ALESSIA

The deposition room is too bright. Not overly harsh, but the kind of natural light that doesn't feel like it belongs here—streaming through high windows as if this were any ordinary meeting and not the final fork in the road for my career, my name, and what little remains of my independence. I sit in the straight-backed chair and lay my palms flat against the table to keep them from shaking. They're already sweating.

Across from me sits a federal judge whose robe is draped loosely over one shoulder. He doesn't look up yet. He's flipping through papers like this is one of a dozen things he has to get through before lunch. To his right, Luca Bernardi. To his left, Elena Greco. Both of them carry clipboards and pens like they're here to take notes, not dissect me inch by inch.

I try not to look at them. I try to keep my eyes on the carafe of water and the single sheet of paper they've placed in front of me—my oath, my name, the date. There's nothing special about this room. There's a vent hissing softly near the door and a clock that clicks every six seconds. There are no cameras watching, no jury seated behind a partition. Only the three of them across the table—and me, sitting alone under the full weight of their scrutiny.

The judge looks up and clears his throat, lifting his chin in my direction. "Let's begin," he says. His voice is brisk and unaffected. The court reporter's fingers begin to fly.

The first questions are simple. My full name. My title. My professional background. I answer them like I'm still a functioning part of the system. Like I haven't compromised the database. Like I'm not here lying by omission.

"Where were you assigned at the time the evidence in question was submitted?" the judge asks, looking up from his file, his voice still even.

I meet his eyes and answer clearly. "The Rome forensic pathology unit." My voice is steady. That surprises me.

"What was your role in processing the sample?" he continues, tapping a pen lightly against the desk.

I take a breath before answering. "I was responsible for DNA extraction and preliminary database alignment."

"And was that done according to protocol?" he asks, one brow lifting slightly as if testing for a crack.

I nod once, letting my hands rest flatter on the table. "Yes."

Dr. Bernardi doesn't look up. Greco's pen scratches faster. The sound is constant, like a metronome driving the pace.

"And your final determination?" the judge prompts, glancing down at the file. "Was the blood found on Matteo Vescari's clothing linked to any known individuals in the criminal database?"

Here it is. The line I've rehearsed a hundred times in the mirror, the line Vincenzo coached me to deliver without flinching.

BEAUTIFUL EVIDENCE

I sit up straighter and say, "No. It was not." But a shiver of shame runs across my spine like a drag racer.

He shifts slightly in his seat. "And is that the final conclusion submitted in your report?"

"Yes." I meet his gaze head-on, not blinking. "That conclusion was recorded and filed in accordance with our protocols."

The silence that follows is measured—heavy without being dramatic. The judge leans back in his chair, slowly folding his hands. Bernardi folds his as well, fingers interlaced. Greco is the one who speaks next, and she narrows her eyes at me as she does it. She's trying to make me crack.

"Ms. Leone, were there any irregularities in the sample collection?" she asks, her tone clipped but polite, her posture sharper than it was a moment ago.

I sit up straighter and answer. "No."

Greco leans forward, her pen still in hand. "No issues with the chain of custody?"

"No," I repeat, keeping my voice flat.

She sets her pen down and lifts her gaze to mine, her eyes narrowing even more. "And to your knowledge, has this sample been altered or interfered with in any way since its collection?"

I hesitate, just long enough to register the trap in her phrasing. A breath barely fills my lungs. The truth presses forward in my mouth, like a cracked filling I can't chew around without bleeding.

"No," I say again, quieter this time, letting my eyes fall briefly to the table.

They shift tactics. Greco leans in, elbows on the table, her expression unreadable. "Why were you the one to complete the analysis?"

I keep my hands flat and my voice level. "I was on shift when the request was entered." I'm not sure why they're asking this. I want to say it was just my job, but I realize they're trying to push me. They want me to confess that I took it because I knew it was connected to my father.

"Were you aware of the implications at the time?" she asks, fingers laced over the folder in front of her.

"I was aware the sample was relevant to an ongoing homicide investigation," I say, my pulse ticking up. "Nothing more."

"Were you aware that the Costa family had been implicated in the murder?" she presses, eyes steady on mine. The chill on my spine sweeps across my arms, to my fingertips, down to my tiptoes. I won't crack.

"Yes," I answer, forcing my voice to remain even.

Greco's tone softens, but the edge remains. "And that your father, Gordo Costa, was affiliated with their organization?" The hammer hits the nail right on the head.

My stomach turns. I've known this question was coming. Vincenzo warned me. I lift my chin slightly.

"I was aware that my father was under investigation," I say carefully. "But I was not in contact with him."

Greco's voice drops a note. "And is your report final?"

"It is," I say, nodding once and leaving it at that. My chest feels like a ticking time bomb, and my palms are so sweaty that if I picked up my glass of water, it would slip from my grasp.

"And you stand by it?" she asks, watching my face closely.

My throat tightens. I nod again, slower this time. "Yes."

The judge clears his throat and closes the folder with a quiet finality. "That concludes the initial deposition," he says, already shifting the next file toward himself. "We reserve the right to call you again should new evidence arise."

The court reporter stops typing. Her hands still hover above the keys.

I rise too quickly from my seat, knees tight, limbs awkward, but I make it out of the room without stumbling. The hallway feels cold, or maybe it's just my anxiety, but I'm sweating too. I move through the building like a ghost and no one stops me to talk.

Outside, the heat slams into me. Rome in early summer is relentless. The pavement radiates warmth through the soles of my shoes, and a line of sweat immediately breaks beneath the collar of my shirt. But the deposition is over, and I am out. It's over.

Across the street, Vincenzo's car is already waiting. He's parked in the shade of a tree, engine running, elbow resting on the windowsill like he hasn't been watching the door for the last hour. I cross without looking at traffic, but the street is quiet. He leans over and opens the door before I reach it. I slide into the passenger seat without a word and close the door behind me.

Vincenzo doesn't say anything right away. He pulls out into traffic, takes a right, then another, winding us away from the state building. I let my head fall back against the seat and close my eyes.

"You held the line," he says after a long silence, and I feel his hand on my knee.

I open my eyes and turn my head toward him. "I did."

"They won't come for you again. They know they don't have proof for any accusation. They wanted an easy win, and you didn't let them win."

Flinching, I swallow the bile of lies back down and nod at him. "They wanted me to flinch… but I did what you told me to do."

"You did so well." He glances at me briefly, then back to the road.

"Then why do I feel so bad inside?" My eyes roll toward the window, and I stare out at the passing scenery.

We drive in silence for a while. My breath starts to slow. My pulse stops kicking at the inside of my throat. I watch the buildings change outside the window, city bleeding into outskirts.

"I'm not like him," I say. I don't mean for it to come out, but it does. Vincenzo doesn't ask who I mean. He knows I mean my father and everything he's done in his life. I won't ever be like him.

"No," he says. "You're not. But you're still his daughter."

The truth of it cuts cleanly, without venom. I let the words settle in my chest. They don't sting or make me flare up in anger. Instead, they settle like truth. They clarify what I've always known but never dared to say out loud.

My phone buzzes in my lap. I glance down and see the name. *Papà.*

There's only one message. One line.

Papà 11:12 AM: You did good, figlia mia.

I stare at it for a long moment, then turn the screen toward Vincenzo.

He reads it and gives a single nod. "It's done."

"No," I say. "It's started..." My hand reaches down to where his rests on my knee, and I interlock our fingers. My future is so uncertain, and nothing I planned or wanted for my life will happen now, but inside, I feel steady. For the first time in my life, I feel like I'm home. And if it takes being connected to the very legacy I tried to cut off to keep myself stable, then so be it.

Because I don't want a future if Enzo isn't in it.

30

VINCENZO

We pull through the outer gate just after noon. Alessia shifts in the passenger seat. She doesn't say anything, but her hands move in her lap like she wants something to hold. I reach across the console and take one, and she lets me. It's the first time she's been back to the Costa compound since she was a kid.

She holds my hand as we park and doesn't let go until I do. We walk in together. Alessia's posture is straight, head high, even if I feel her pulse ticking fast through our joined hands.

"You okay?" I ask her. This is old hat to me. I've been here multiple times a day for most of my life. But Alessia's pure heart is different from mine, and since she broke ties a long time ago, this place has been nothing but a memory to her.

"Yeah," she says, nodding, but I see the apprehension on her face as I lead her through the wide double doors into the foyer.

In the dining room, Emilio's already seated at the head of the long table. Food hasn't been served yet, but there are three place settings, glasses of water poured halfway, and cloth napkins pressed into perfect folds at every plate. The table feels curated and intentional. He's making a statement that I wonder if Alessia understands. This isn't family yet, but he's trying.

Emilio straightens his spine and stands when we enter, his eyes steady and unreadable. "Alessia," he says. He lets out a quiet breath, sizing her up like a man measuring an opponent, not his niece. "You look like your father." His tongue clicks disapprovingly. I know it's been ages since he saw her, but he can't be surprised that she looks like Gordo. They share the same DNA.

She doesn't flinch. She lifts one eyebrow, a flicker of dry amusement breaking through her nerves. "I'll take that as a compliment." I feel the humor in her tone, given that Emilo and Gordo share a striking resemblance themselves.

Emilio gestures to the seat at his right. He eases back into his seat and nods once. "It is one." We sit. She takes the seat beside Emilio. I take the one across from her.

He studies her for a long moment before speaking again. "You've done a lot these past few weeks." His gruff tone makes me stiffen, but he follows that with, "You did well," and I try to relax a little.

Alessia folds her hands in her lap. She speaks without the slightest hesitation. "I did what I had to."

Emilio nods and the corner of his mouth twitches. "I don't doubt that." Reaching for his water, he says, "But I didn't bring you here to rehash decisions. I brought you because you made them. And now you live with what comes next."

"And that is?" I ask with an edge of protection to my tone. He knows how I feel about this woman and since the moment we walked in, he's been sizing her up. His eyes flick to mine, and I see no malice, after all this time and the way he planned to kill her. Finally, Emilio has let his anger with his brother go. He won't carry forward the vendetta to Gordo's daughter.

He leans forward, hands clasped in front of him. "You're free," he says. "No one here expects anything from you. Not after what you did. You want to disappear? You can. You want to go back to your science? We'll make sure no one questions your credentials."

Alessia's eyes narrow slightly. She tilts her head, testing the space between what's offered and what's owed. "And if I want something else?"

Emilio shrugs lightly, but there's nothing casual in the way he watches her face. "There's a seat here if you want it. We don't offer that lightly, but you earned your way in." He sighs. "Vincenzo tells me you may be interested in more…"

She glances at me, but I see the question tucked beneath it. I nod once, letting her know she's not alone but also that this is her moment. I won't step in. I won't speak for her.

She turns back to Emilio and leans back, her fingers tracing the edge of her glass without lifting it. "I always thought if I left forensic work, I'd do something quieter. You know… bake bread… teach undergrads. Anything that didn't come with NDAs and bulletproof glass."

He chuckles under his breath, shaking his head. "Not quite what your father had in mind, I imagine."

She breathes in and lets it out slowly. "I'm not sure he had anything in mind for me at all," she says, but there's no bitterness in it.

I study her across the table and marvel at how absolutely stunning she is and how she captivates the room. "I want…" Alessia's soft sigh meets me where my heart pinches.

"I want to stay exactly where I am," she says, her voice low but clear, meant only for me. I reach for her hand across the table and wrap my fingers around hers. "With Enzo… And I want my family." Her eyes are sharp as she says, "I just don't want to be involved in the crime."

Emilio grins in pride as if Alessia is his own daughter and she has made him proud. "I think we can arrange that." He nods at the doorway and the staff comes in, setting out a feast on the table in front of us.

Lunch is casual. Emilio talks about Gordo and Rosa, how he misses them and how his life has taken them all in different directions. He tells her how honored he is to have her home and assures her that my work won't keep me from tending to her needs. When lunch is complete, he calls his staff back.

Once the staff clears the table, Emilio wipes his mouth with his napkin and sets it neatly beside his untouched plate. He checks his watch, then looks up.

"There's one more thing," he says, rising slowly. His tone is less formal now, but still measured. "You'll want to take this next part on the terrace." There is a hint of sparkle in his eyes that's not normal for him, and I'm curious to see what he has planned for us.

Alessia stands before I do. I lead her through the back hall, out past the garden as we follow Emilio. The terrace overlooks the western ridge, where the hills flatten and the sky opens up. A phone is already waiting on the small stone table, a video call incoming.

Emilio points at it and smiles, saying, "It's for you," and she reaches for it like it might burn her.

Gordo's face appears when she swipes to answer, and she glances up at me with confusion. The signal's strong. He's in a room with shuttered windows and a leather chair. Somewhere safe.

He looks older than the last time I saw him but clearer. Like the noise around him has settled and he feels more at peace. Gordo leans slightly toward the screen, eyes sharp but warm. "Alessia," he says, and he draws it out in a fatherly way. "*Figlia mia...*"

She sits slowly, and I stay behind her, with one hand on the back of her chair and my fingertips brushing her shoulder.

He shifts in his chair, glancing briefly off-screen before refocusing. "I saw the transcript," Gordo says. "I know what you did." His head bobs in one continuous nod, and I shift my hand to her shoulder, squeezing it.

Alessia presses her lips together. Her voice stays level, but her hands fold together. "I didn't really do it for you."

Gordo's head drops slowly, but when he looks back up, something proud flickers in his expression. "I know." He nods. "But you did it for the right reasons. You did it for family."

She doesn't respond to him, but Gordo doesn't push. He looks at her with a kind of softness not often seen in a man like him. "I'm proud of you. That's all. I just wanted you to hear it."

The screen goes black, *Call ended* flashing in bright white letters, and her hand rises to touch mine, still perched on her shoulder. She sets the phone down and exhales slowly. The air dusts my fingers as she turns to kiss my knuckles.

Behind us, Emilio leans against the doorframe, arms folded, his posture more reflective than guarded.

"You needed that?" I say quietly.

She nods, and her fingers curl around mine again. "I didn't realize how much."

The terrace goes quiet except for the breeze shifting through the vines. She stands and wraps her arms around me.

I pull her closer. "Whatever comes next, we'll face it together."

For the first time, I don't feel like I'm protecting her. I feel like she's standing beside me. Not as someone who needs rescuing, but as someone who belongs here. With me.

31

EPILOGUE: ALESSIA

The anchorman's voice drifts from the small TV mounted above the stove and music plays in the kitchen—something Enzo is using his speaker and phone to play. I don't pay close attention to what the anchorman is saying until I catch my own name. It's quiet—tucked between mentions of the 416-bis case backlog and the upcoming elections—but it's there. My name scrolls across the ticker, tied to discredited evidence and a procedural collapse. The charges tied to the investigation have been dismissed entirely.

I stare at the screen for a few seconds longer with my mug half-lifted in my hand. Then I take a sip of my tea and exhale slowly. The salty air slips in through the open windows, curling around my bare legs and stirring the hem of my robe.

Vincenzo hums behind me, moving between the stove and the fridge. He's barefoot, shirtless, hair still damp from his morning swim. He cracks another egg against the skillet and tips it in with practiced ease.

"You hear that?" I ask, nodding toward the screen.

He glances over his shoulder. "Something about Bernardi?"

I lower the volume, then turn to face him fully. "The case collapsed. They're blaming him for evidence tampering. Internal Affairs has launched an investigation."

He slides a spatula under the eggs and flips them. "Hmm." Am I wrong to love how amazing he looks in that pair of dark shorts with his hair mussed? Am I wrong to want to melt into his strength and be happy that the mess of my life has turned into something so amazing the past few months?

"Hmm?" I raise a brow. "That's all you have to say?"

He shrugs, not even trying to look innocent. "I told you it'd work out."

I cross my arms and lean against the counter. "Vincenzo."

He doesn't answer right away, just plates the eggs and adds a sprinkle of sea salt before sliding them onto the table. When he finally meets my eyes, there's no smugness in his expression, just quiet satisfaction.

"You asked me to protect your name," he says. "I did."

"And how many strings did you pull?"

He picks up a slice of toast and bites into it. "Enough."

I shake my head but I'm smiling. Months ago, I would've pressed harder. Would've demanded every detail, every contact, every ethical boundary he danced over. Now I let it go, because when your filthy rich boyfriend invites you to a week on the Spanish coast, you don't question how he makes his money.

I let it go because we're here. Because it's over. Because the sun spills through the curtain-less windows and the world, for once, doesn't feel like it's chasing us.

I sit across from him and spoon a bit of marmalade onto my plate. My appetite's been strange lately—ravenous one minute, queasy the next. This morning, it's the latter. I take one bite of egg and excuse myself, murmuring something about needing a sweater. The hall feels longer than usual. The bathroom feels colder, especially the tile as my knees hit the ground and I worship the porcelain goddess yet again. It's been happening more frequently, and I know it can only mean one thing.

When I return to the kitchen, Vincenzo looks up the second I step into the doorway. His fork pauses midair.

"What is it?" he asks.

I sit down slowly. "I, uh… I missed my period." My head stays down so he can't see the small smile I'm holding back. I bite my lip as he sets his fork down. I expect a dozen reactions. Questions. Worry. Disbelief. But what I get is silence as he studies me for a long moment, then leans across the table.

"Are you sure?" he asks me, and with his eyebrows raised like that, I can tell he is excited by the thought.

"I haven't tested yet, but it's been long enough that I noticed, and it's not like me."

He reaches for my hand. His thumb brushes my knuckles as the grin stretches over his lips. "I'm going to be a father?" he asks, dipping his head, and I chuckle for a moment.

"I think so, yes…"

The ecstatic "Whoop!" he releases almost startles me, and then he stands, jubilantly hoisting me off the ground and spinning me around a few times. It's dizzying, and I have to cling to him when my feet touch back down on the cold tile.

When Enzo's lips cover mine, it's hot and passionate. He kisses me like the last few months have all been leading to this exact second. His hands frame my face firmly, and his mouth moves over mine with a hunger that sends heat curling through me. When we break apart, we're both breathless.

But he doesn't let me go. His forehead rests against mine. "You really think there's a baby?" he asks, softer now, as if the first time I told him

BEAUTIFUL EVIDENCE

he didn't believe it and he needs to hear it over again to make sure it's real.

I nod slowly. "I do. I've never been late before like this."

We just stay like that for a moment—chests touching, hearts in sync, like the storm we weathered never touched us at all. He wraps his arms fully around me and holds me to himself like he can already feel the change in the air, in my body, in us.

"I didn't think life would look like this," I murmur, pressing my cheek to his chest. "I thought if I survived, I'd have to spend the rest of it looking over my shoulder."

He strokes my back. "No one's going to touch you now."

"And if I am pregnant?" I ask. "What then?"

His hand settles protectively at the small of my back. "Then we make space for that future. We find a bigger place. You let me build a nursery. I learn how to install car seats and argue with you about names."

I laugh warmly. "You'd argue?"

He pulls back just enough to look at me. "Only if you suggest something ridiculous. Like Zeus. Or Vito." He tickles my side, and I squeal while pushing him away.

"Vito?" I wrinkle my nose. "You're really going to take that risk?"

He leans in and kisses my temple. "We'll figure it out. You and me. We always do."

The music from the little Bluetooth speaker near the counter changes tracks, something lazy and warm drifting into the kitchen. He lifts an eyebrow. "Dance with me."

"It's nine in the morning," I say, laughing.

He's already pulling me toward the open space between the stove and table. "Then it's as good a time as any."

We sway together, barefoot on cold tile, my arms around his neck and his around my waist. He hums against my hair. I'm not thinking about the headlines, or the past, or the wreckage we climbed out of. I'm thinking about the way his thumb strokes my side. About how right it feels.

He leans back a little. "Alessia?"

"Mmm?"

"When we get married," he says, and there's no hesitation in his voice, "your father's walking you down the aisle."

I blink at him. "First of all, is that a proposal?" I ask, snickering. Then I say, "What if he doesn't want to?"

"Then I'll go find him myself and convince him." He grins. "Emilio can sulk in the corner and call him names. I don't care."

"You're serious?"

He kisses me again, softer this time. "Dead serious. I don't want a wedding without you walking toward me with the people who made you standing behind you. We'll do it right."

Tears press at the back of my eyes, but I don't let them fall. Somehow, this man understands the word *family* more than I ever have, and I have so much to learn from him.

Because this—this is what it means to choose a future. Not with perfect safety. Not with clean hands. But with open eyes and both feet planted, finally, on solid ground.

Printed in Dunstable, United Kingdom